Many Believable Lies
What you don't know ...

Joseph McConnell

ProcArch LLC, Ann Arbor

ISBN: 978-0-9886913-6-0

Third edition, Paperback, 2015.

The quotations from Hesiod are from the beautiful and witty Stanley Lombardo translation of the Theogony, published in 1993 by Hackett Publishing Company. Reproduced by permission of the publisher.

This is a work of fiction. With the exception of Mac MacArthur, who is in some ways a physical and psychological echo of the author, all characters in this work are fictional, and they do not represent real people. The Ann Arbor Police Department and the County of Washtenaw do not have personnel such as those described here nor are the procedural details necessarily accurate. There is no such town as Rome, Michigan, and although there is a Sturgis and a Sturgis Police Department, the officers depicted here have no basis in reality.

This book is for Linda who knew when to help, and it's dedicated to the memory of Coney Dog, a heart dog if there ever was one. Thanks to Ken Pardiac for general aviation clues, the folks at Bearclaw Coffee for keeping me caffeinated, and to oncologists everywhere for fighting an uphill battle.

Many Believable Lies

*And they once taught Hesiod the art of singing verse
While he pastured his lambs on holy Helikon's slopes.
And this was the very first thing they told me,
The Olympian Muses, daughters of Zeus Aegisholder.
"Hillbillies and bellies, poor excuses for shepherds:
We know how to tell many believable lies,
But also, when we want to, how to speak the plain
truth."*

It was still cold for April. A hard winter and an unwilling spring, MacArthur thought, then wondered where he'd gotten that phrase. Something he read, probably. From that thought to "something I ate" was no long jump, given the more or less constant nausea. But it wasn't, of course, anything he ate, it was something — or everything together — that he'd swallowed: maintenance doses of eight different drugs. Another phrase, one he knew was original, came to mind: cancer is inconvenient.

At least he could drive again. And he was, stopping at the drive-through at the coffee shop nearest to his house, a shop perched on the triangular corner where Stadium and Washtenaw split. The baristas knew him, knew his usual order, and knew, vaguely, that he was some sort of cop. "Some sort, right." The kind on disability leave, that would be. Not officially on any roster, not uniformed. Theoretically out of the loop. Theory and practice weren't always in alignment, of course, but plenty of things, from the city's insurance policies to the Social Security Administration's definition of 'disabled', meant that he no longer had any demonstrable connection with the Ann Arbor police department.

Which meant by extension that when something unusual happened, he could help out, but with everyone looking the other way. MacArthur had a retiree identification card and a concealed weapon license, and that was about it, that and nearly twenty years' experience in investigation.

A blast of wind and cold rain hit the car as he drove back out onto Stadium. Traffic was backed up too far from the light, making a left turn inadvisable. No matter; he'd just go right, left onto Saint Francis, and back through the neighborhoods to his house. As he signaled the turn, his cell phone rang. Not a fan of distracted drivers in general and with no particular need to hurry home, he pulled over, stopped, and fished the phone out of a jacket pocket. Caller ID told him who it was.

A month before, in even more unpleasant weather, a large group of FBI agents and Michigan State Police troopers had assembled in a cell phone lot at the south end of Detroit/Wayne Metropolitan Airport. DTW is one of the few important things located in the city of Rome, Michigan, and it was a handy staging area for a large drug raid. There were no members of the Rome Police Department present, since it was their headquarters and the home of their chief that were going to be raided. By the end of the day, seven officers, the chief, and a city council member were under arrest, charged with conspiracies of various kinds in the movement of cocaine into Detroit. The deal was an old classic: the high bidder was ignored by the local police, while others were suppressed. The paying customers didn't have to resort to violence among themselves; violent crimes, if they happened, wouldn't tend to happen in Rome; the local department looked good on paper; and a percentage of the drugs that tried to come in through Metro moved smoothly from the airport out of town and off to that unfortunate big city to the east. The mules had to get by the TSA, of course, and the limited DEA presence, but once they were out the door, the drugs could go quickly and safely to safe houses.

2

It all unraveled, predictably, when one of the bought-in traffickers was arrested by another department. The product had to move on from Rome, of course, and an unlucky traffic stop in Taylor, just a bit to the east, caught a low-ranking player with a kilo of the stuff. He didn't immediately cave in, but he did start out by insisting that the arresting officers call his 'friend'. His friend, obviously, was a Rome cop who was supposed to be a contact point in case something went wrong. The Taylor officers were smart enough to call the FBI, instead.

After a while and after a lot of pointed questions, it dawned on the druggie that a) his insurance coverage didn't extend outside Rome and, b) he was personally screwed. He promptly rolled over on everything he knew about the Rome police agreement, but he said nothing of any value about his colleagues and sources; that, after all, could get him killed, in or out of prison.

But a dirty cop case was almost as good, from a PR standpoint, as taking down drug importers. The arrestee's information was the basis of a brief, covert investigation, and it was closely held until the federal and state agencies were ready to move. Afterwards, it was all over the local news, and improbable as it might seem, that was the first that most of the non-paying drug players knew about it.

They knew they'd had a hard time with the Rome cops, but they didn't know the extent to which the deck had been stacked against them. Now they knew, and they were pissed. But on this miserable April morning, the buzz in the press had died down, people with one opinion or the other about the integrity of local police forces had gotten tired of commenting on blogs or looking for ways to blame the Obama administration, and in general, it was yesterday's news. MacArthur had only passing interest in the whole thing; he didn't know anybody on the Rome force. Neither the AAPD nor their most closely cooperating agency, the Washtenaw County

Sheriff's Department, had any involvement, and the only consensus among the officers was a general disgust for the bad cops in question. It was not on Mac's mind at all as he answered his phone call.

MacArthur's phone told him that 'JL' was calling, and from her personal cell. That usually meant one of two things: to see if he could join a few of the old guard for lunch or to see if he could take a look at something unusual and spooky. When he answered, Detective Jennifer Langton said, "Hi, Mac. Saw something interesting on the net. I'll send it to you. It's about the airport."

Something interesting was part of their trivial code; it meant "Can you come and look at this?" And the airport could only mean the Ann Arbor airport. Nothing else in the way of an airport would be the AAPD's concern. The city owned it, even though it jutted out into Pittsfield Township, south of Ellsworth Road. So something out there wouldn't be a simple property crime or a domestic dispute. It'd be something interesting — unusual and spooky.

And she bore Chimaira

> *And she bore Chimaira who breathed raging fire,*
> *And she was dreadful and huge and fast and strong*
> *And she had three heads: one of a green-eyed lion,*
> *One of a goat, and one of a serpent ...*

The Ann Arbor airport was a small general aviation field. Corporate and private planes used it, and various media blimps and helicopters dropped in for University of Michigan football games. There had been occasional proposals for expansion, but no one could make a good case for it. It was bounded by State Street and Ellsworth on the east and north and private property on the west and south, and lengthening the runways to take even small jets proved controversial and difficult to achieve. So this morning, especially with the poor weather, it wasn't exactly congested with aircraft. Ariel Suleiman was motivated, though. She was a new pilot, and she was going to do some flying today, regardless. Some practice in cross winds and light rain wouldn't hurt; it was only blowing twelve knots, anyway, with the wind out of the east. It was Tuesday, April tenth.

She did her preflight walk-around on the Cessna 152 she was leasing. The wind and rain were actually a good thing, she told herself. *I need to fly on marginal days, too.* Convinced that nothing had fallen off or gone flat or drained out since the last time she'd been up, she got into the cabin, ran down the starting drill, and kicked off the engine. With the gauges settled into nominal territory, she called the tower. "Ann Arbor Ground; Cessna 1517 Juliet at the Northwest Tees with Delta; taxi active runway." *With Delta* meant she'd already listened to a weather broadcast.

The tower told her to go ahead and taxi to runway six. Six was the strip that would take her east, up and out over State Street. When she got out there, she ran over the engine settings. Fuel Mixture: rich, throttle run up to 1800 RPM, both magnetos on, carburetor heat on, oil pressure okay. She throttled back to idle and made sure the trim tabs were set.

"Ann Arbor Tower; Cessna 17 Juliet ready for take-off runway six, northeast bound."

The tower replied, "Cessna 17 Juliet cleared for takeoff, runway six, straight out departure."

"Cleared for takeoff, 17 Juliet," Ariel acknowledged, and opened the throttle.

If ever there was a proven design, the Cessna qualified for honors. It wasn't a performance plane, but it certainly fulfilled its objectives: it got you off the ground and set you back down again, with a high probability of the latter being in one piece. As Ariel gathered speed, she eased the yoke back and lifted the aircraft off the pavement. She'd done this many times before, and the landscape below was unexceptional. With the plane's high wing out of the way of the view, she'd seen a lot of the Ann Arbor landscape. This time, though, something was off. The airport was required to have an obstacle-free area extending three hundred feet beyond the runway, and this morning there was an obstacle. The obstacle looked a hell of a lot like a person, lying quite still.

Ariel got the aircraft steady on her outbound course and tried to decide if she'd seen what she thought she saw. She was not ex-military, had not flown reconnaissance, had been trained, in fact, to focus on flying and not on sightseeing. However, there wasn't supposed to be anything out there in the grass but grass. So she called the tower again: "Ann Arbor tower; Cessna 17 Juliet return for touch-and-go runway six."

The tower agreed, uncharacteristically letting her go left over the city and not right, over industrial parks and cornfields. She banked left, swinging north over the Briarwood Mall, out past the freeway ramp at Ann Arbor/Saline Road and I-94, and back east over the airport. On the second pass over the field, she was sure. Someone was lying still, about halfway between the end of the runway and State Street, with one arm flung out to the side. Ariel picked up the microphone again.

The rivers near which they dwell

> *... many other rivers, chattering as they flow,*
> *Sons of Ocean that lady Tethys bore,*
> *But it is hard for a mortal to tell all their names.*
> *People know the rivers near which they dwell.*

One of the things about Mac MacArthur was that he worked hard at not looking like a cop. Or a retired cop, for that matter. He'd gotten into the State Police academy at a time when it was unfashionable, recruiting was a challenge, and physical requirements were relaxed. He was not a big guy. Looking back, he wondered how he'd managed to survive patrol work for six years without getting his ass kicked more than that one time. And even then, he'd managed to take the drunken jackass down and cuff him before another car got there. Pure luck — the guy was too drunk to fight effectively after he'd gotten in his initial sucker punch, and Mac had broken away, stepped back one pace, and fractured the kid's collarbone with a baton strike. The good old man-powered Taser.

His time as a state trooper was mostly stunningly boring work involving driving up and down freeways, dinging people for speeding. Hanging over your head was the threat of being assigned to one of Michigan's many failing industrial cities; for a while, the State Police took over freeway enforcement in Detroit, simply because the locals couldn't cope. And if you got promoted too far, in the wrong track, you'd just end up investigating your fellow officers for shootings, beatings, corruption. It got to look more and more unpleasant. He'd made up his mind to go for something more variable and a little more directly related to public safety, something more diverse. He hadn't yet heard the old Scott Adams line about diversity — the longer you work here, the more diverse it gets — but it was seeming to him to be true about the State Police, so he applied for a patrol job in Ann Arbor. In hindsight, he considered it the best decision he'd ever made.

For one thing, he met his wife. Early on, he and another officer were on foot patrol in the downtown area, the old downtown, centered around Main and Liberty. Less focused on student trade, the blocks just west of Main were heavy with bars and restaurants, some of them for tourists and parents and never a source of problems (except for the health inspectors), and some of them largely patronized by locals; *they* could have issues from time to time. The two cops had walked down Liberty between Main and Ashley, sticking their heads into the various places, "sniffing," as his older colleague put it, for trouble. As they came to the last place on the block, the door opened and four people came out, one of whom stumbled coming down the steps. Mac reached out and steadied her and asked if she was all right.

"Yes," she said. "I'm fine. I'm the only one who *hasn't* been drinking."

A year later, via an improbable series of coincidental meetings and "Who's that woman over there at the back table?" introductions, Mac and Colleen got married. Mac chalked this up to a kind of luck; things seemed to work out for him. He'd never considered himself the Olympian ideal of manhood, and he often wondered why any woman, given a choice, would look twice. Colleen, on the other hand, was lively and cheerful and attractive and in every way an ideal partner. She was also hooked into Ann Arbor's early Internet businesses. Police work paid as badly as it always did, but Colleen went on to build a career with, if not quite executive compensation, at least pay and perks half again as comfortable as Mac's. Instead of living in a peripheral town, Ypsilanti or Dexter or Chelsea, Mac and Colleen were able to afford Ann Arbor prices and taxes. And Mac was able to rationalize it as making him a better Ann Arbor cop; he had skin in the game, he was an Ann Arborite himself.

He'd moved into investigation when there was an opening; his supervisor prompted him to do it, recognizing that sheer physical prowess and stamina weren't ever going to be Mac's strong suits. Maybe patrol isn't the best place for a short guy, even if he did come out of the state academy. He made detective in a little less than the usual time, did some good work on cases that involved other agencies, and gradually became the department's informal expert on cooperating with the FBI, DEA, and other ozone-based federal life forms. Now he was semi-retired, and nobody with any insight into physiology and disease staging would place a large bet on his returning to work. Even the government agreed, giving him a small amount of social security disability. Nothing is ever guaranteed with the government, but when it was approved they told Mac, in effect, that they'd likely audit his claim in fifteen years or so. That was the most optimistic assessment of his lifespan Mac had heard since his diagnosis, and it actually cheered him up.

But there were still these tricky cases; the AAPD was not immune to the budget axes being wielded everywhere in the state, and they'd elected not to fill his position, blithely holding it open for his return, though nobody expected him to come back. Because the downtown foot patrols had been canceled some years ago, the panhandlers and hobos and eccentric characters were a growing feature, up and down Main and Liberty and Washington. It was pretty clear to everyone that when Mac finally pulled the pin, the slot would be used to add a patrol officer, not a new detective. So when one of the remaining investigative people took on a weird report, there was a polite disregard for *de jure* disability and a very much *de facto* approach to getting his advice. Jenn Langton's quick phone call translated directly into, "Got a funny one. Can you help? Out at the airport."

Another of Mac's techniques for not looking like a cop was to drive an inconspicuous car, more accurately a small Nissan pickup. Four-wheel drive made it almost unstoppable in the usually moderate snow of southeastern Michigan (God help you if you were over in Grand Rapids, on the west side of the state. Lake effect snow hammered the place for months on end, but it spared the East Coast, by and large). The truck looked highly mainstream but was quietly tailored for Mac's purposes, with a scanner and radio and a large lock box in the bed for gear. No lightbars, obviously; no reason, since you don't do traffic stops in your personal vehicle. He did have a magnetic roof flasher, just to establish it as a cop's car, but these days, he tried to park in civilian spaces and not on people's lawns. He looked essentially like a tradesman, and he

9

fostered that notion by dressing like one. Most days, for example, if you took even a second look as he went by, you'd see a short guy in a ball cap driving it, wearing glasses and a camouflage army surplus M-65 jacket. Mac had never served a day in the armed forces, but the venerable old M-65 was a staple of the long-haired set during his stint at the University, and a recent fit of nostalgia had driven him to get another. It felt heavy and familiar and comforting, unlike nylon and down parkas, and it was stiff enough that no amount of belt-carried equipment under it would show recognizable profiles on the outside.

And that was important, because Mac, out and about, was something of an arsenal. His personal sidearm over most of his career had been a short .38 revolver, but in the last few years, he'd switched to a Glock subcompact, a brutal-looking little automaton, solid black and holding eleven rounds of nine millimeter. When he'd gotten it (as a Christmas present from Colleen, actually), he'd deliberately set out to find a flaw and couldn't. It shot any sort of cheap range ammunition perfectly, hundreds of rounds after hundreds of rounds, and it did the same with high-end defense cartridges. It was heavier than the Smith & Wesson it replaced, but it was a distinct improvement.

That gun lived on his belt, high up behind the right hip. In warmer weather, when he was wearing a jacket that suited it, it could be in a breast pocket. He'd have a couple of additional magazines somewhere, varying with the clothes he had on. There was always a flashlight, usually the kind with a striking surface; a pair of handcuffs; and locked in the box in the truck, a Ruger Mini-14 rifle with a composite stock and a short range electronic sight. There was a Type II body armor vest in the box, as well. Add to that a wallet, keys, a pocket knife, a Leatherman combination tool, and a cell phone, and you can understand why he had to give up and wear suspenders, just to keep his pants from falling down. Not many people knew the extent of his, shall we say, preparedness, but it stemmed from one simple thing; AAPD had no separate special weapons unit. No backup he could call in would be much better armed than he was, and so he'd done in recent years what he'd always done when he could get away with it: bought his own gear with his own money.

Mac turned south off Ellsworth Road and parked the truck in the airport's parking lot. There was a marked car there, of course, and a patrol officer he knew. The young man hadn't been on the force long, but he knew enough to know that when Mac showed up at a crime scene, it was always by invitation, and it always meant an unusual situation.

Mac greeted him with a wave and a very typical cop salutation, "What have we got?" He didn't attempt to walk any farther, brush the officer off, or show any inclination to pull rank. He didn't have any to pull, after all.

"Homicide, it looks like. A body, anyway. Down at the east end of the runway."

"Really? Jennifer here somewhere?" Mac asked. He was already well along the continuum from minor to intense interest. The number of plausible ways a body could be where the boy was pointing were narrowing quickly.

"Detective Langton? I'll call her, tell her you're here," said the officer, demonstrating good sense and a truly professional ability to suppress curiosity when required. Mac stood quietly by while a call took place.

"She's going to drive back here and pick you up. It's a long walk down there," the kid said, and Mac heard the underlying addition: "for an old sick guy." But on balance, he'd take the ride. It *was* a long walk, in fact any walk was a long one these days. It was cold and raining and his legs hurt — all his damn joints hurt, in fact, and he huddled himself into the field jacket with a grateful sense of its protection. After a few seconds, he said, "Be right back," and went back to the truck. He swapped the ball cap for a broad-brimmed, waterproof boonie hat from the lock box. As he locked things back up, Langton's car pulled up on the other side of the yellow tape, with another patrol officer driving. Mac nodded to the kid on duty, said hello to the guy in the car, and got in. The officer didn't seem surprised at picking up a damp old man dressed like an unemployed mercenary. He just said, "Jennifer asked me to come get you."

As they turned around, another car pulled up, one that Mac recognized as belonging to an assistant Medical Examiner from the County ME's office down on Ingalls Street; Ann Arbor being the county seat, all that subsidiary officialdom was conveniently close at hand. The two vehicles proceeded in convoy down the runway toward a small group of people standing around something on the ground. Beyond it, Mac could see cops stringing yellow tape along the road and around a gate, quite a long way off to the right. There were patrol cars parked on State Street, too.

Elektra

> And Thaumas married deep flowing Ocean's
> Daughter Elektra, who bore swift Iris and
> The rich-haired Harpies, Aello and Okypetes ...

Jenn Langton was not a happy person this morning nor most mornings, for that matter. For one thing, her family situation wasn't soothing. Both parents were recently dead, as was her marriage to a county sheriff's deputy. That marriage had produced one miscarriage and then two completely unmanageable daughters; nothing about any of it — any aspect of her family — was a supportive backdrop to a detective's career. In fact, she was on the AAPD simply because it was a move out of daily contact with her ex-husband; otherwise, she'd still be processing inmates at the Washtenaw County jail.

The girls were impossible. At an early age, before the marriage ended, they'd been hard to read, sometimes loving and attached to their parents, sometimes off in some kind of personal inner demonhood, haunting one or the other parent, each other, or a peer from school about whom Jenn and her husband would have never heard until some irate administrator complained about a disturbance. There was never any classifiable reason for the likes and dislikes the girls took to people. They weren't homophobes or racists (unlike their father, who was both), nor were they snobs or anti-snobs. There was just no telling who they'd conflict with.

After the divorce, things went completely south. Until they reached eighteen, the girls nominally lived with Jenn — she had nominal custody — but on the order of once a month, one of them would take off to live with Dad. These changes lasted less than forty-eight hours, typically, since Dad was a much more skilled ass-kicker than Mom. He'd even handcuffed one of them, once, for having some marijuana and — this was the real objection — leaving it around in his condo. Jenn never arrested them or reported them, since she had a very sharp set of opinions about the effectiveness of the judicial system in correcting behavior. She didn't have any better ideas, but she didn't see jail as doing them any good, either.

However, one or the other girl was always being brought home by a sympathetic cop or actually detained, usually for shoplifting or being in a car with some boy or group of boys who were drunk, stoned, creating a disturbance, or all three. Both had narrowly, very narrowly, skated by drug charges more than once, mostly through professional courtesy; they were just smart enough to keep from committing misdemeanors outside the county. They were now both out of Jenn's house, thank God, but no less a nightmare or pair of nightmares than they'd even been. One was in a clearly abusive relationship with a guy from Dearborn. Jenn had never met him, but she'd

13

seen his handiwork in the form of a nice set of black eyes and a missing tooth. The other girl was hypothetically unattached, but had a suspiciously large disposable income, expensive if tasteless taste in clothing and friends, and a massive attitude. Jenn's worst, most recurring bad dream was that she'd get a call in the middle of the night announcing that one or the other of the girls was dead or pregnant.

When Jenn moved up into investigation, Mac was assigned as a sort of mentor and guardian. Early on, she mishandled a situation with the FBI on a case, and Mac managed to straighten out the resulting memo war and general ill-feeling. Now, she was gun shy of anything touchy or complicated or even mysterious unless she could get Mac to look over her shoulder and make sure she wasn't violating some unwritten rule (written rules, she could handle; she'd have made a good attorney, in fact). At the bottom of it was the sure knowledge that she needed to keep her job. Fortyish and not especially glamorous, she expected to be single the rest of her life and to have to go on coddling her offspring. Even a day or two suspended without pay would be a problem, and she saw Mac as a way of double-checking her actions to avoid giving any kind of departmental offense.

Logically, this meant that she liked simple cases where getting the paperwork right was more critical than catching the criminals. Her favorite case of the moment was one in which, following Horace Greeley's advice, a young man had gone west, travelling the whole six and a half miles from the south side of Ypsilanti to Ann Arbor, where he held up a bank. He just walked in without any mask or other disguise and asked for money; no guns, bombs, anthrax, or anything else were implied. Then, while being observed by bank employees and customers, he walked a block away and got on a bus for Ypsi. Since radio (or in fact pony express) was faster than Ann Arbor Transit Authority buses, he was met by the Ypsilanti police and taken into custody. Langton's involvement was all after the fact, all procedural, all comradely interface with other agencies. There were no questions about actual guilt or innocence, motive, means, and all that. She hadn't had to kick anyone's ass, and nobody was kicking hers. What happened to the young Nobel laureate later on was a matter for the courts, and all she had to do was make sure the facts were impeccably clear and correctly reported.

On the other hand, cases like this damn thing at the airport were scary. She could screw it up, of course; that was a real possibility. More to the point, it reminded her that the body could have been one of her daughters. Random death or any kind of random happening was not a comfortable thing for Jenn.

Consequently, she was very glad to see Mac when he got out of her car, slowly and with a curse or two as weight transferred from his hips to his legs. She was glad to see him, yes, but he looked like hell, and her relief was replaced with a moment of quiet panic at the apparently limited time in which she'd still have the benefit of his advice.

"Hi, Jenn," Mac said. "What've we got?" The old formula.

"Mac! Thanks for coming. Sorry to get you out in the rain. Could be an interesting one, though," she said. There was that code word again: *interesting*.

"No problem. I was out already, getting my coffee. Is there just the one?"

"Yeah, just one body. Lying like this, drag marks. They came in over there, cut the lock off a gate."

Mac looked in the direction she was pointing, and he saw that there was a large, vehicle-sized gate in the State Street fence, designed to let trailered planes come in and be dropped off at one of the small hangars south of the operational area. "Last night?" he asked.

"Yeah," Langton told him. "The first plane to take off this morning saw him. Pretty visible place."

"Not too concerned with hiding it, then?" Now what would that imply? Mac's curiosity instantly bubbled up that question. You typically dump a body any old where to get rid of it fast, or you buy yourself some time by dumping it somewhere it won't be found for a while. This was not an easy, obscure, nor especially safe place to do any of that. Just one patrol car coming by on State Street or even a curious civilian would ruin your evening.

The ME's assistant had been getting his gear out of the car, and now he walked up to Jenn, needing to know who to work with. "Hi, Langton," he said. "You in charge of this one?"

"Yes, unfortunately. Have a ball. We've looked around pretty well for tracks, empties, and all that, so you're up. Over to you."

"You got all the pictures you need?" He sounded uncertain, but this particular kid was always more interested in taking digital snaps than actually touching bodies, as Mac well knew.

"Oh, yes, we're all set. It's your body," said Jenn. "No ID yet, though. Nothing like a wallet that we could see."

"Okay, I'm on it," he said, and started away.

"We didn't turn him over," Jenn told Mac, "but there's a clear pair of gunshot wounds in the back of the head, nothing else visible."

"A pair?"

"Yes, two separate shots, one from the right rear, one from the left. Medium caliber handguns, if I had to say."

"Standing? Kneeling?"

"I don't know. If I had to guess, probably from above, like he was on the ground. I couldn't tell if his hands were tied or anything."

"Well, that's all ME stuff, anyway," said Mac. "And you said no ID, right?"

"Right, not in his back pockets, anyway. We didn't move him."

Mac strolled over to the body and stood behind the ME. The victim looked young, quite young, in fact. He was clearly a black male or else a female doing a good job of presenting as male. He was lying on his face, with the left arm outstretched and the right tucked under the body. He had on a gray hoodie with no logo or anything else on the back, and his trousers were slightly unusual for his age and presumable social group: olive drab cargo pants. He was barefoot, no socks or shoes, and nothing was making any interesting bulges from under the clothing. If there was anything in those pants pockets, it wasn't large. Mac couldn't tell if there was a belt; the hoodie came down below the waist. Everything was soaked by the rain.

The left wrist was sticking out of his sleeve, and Mac stepped just a bit closer, trying not to intrude on or interfere with the assistant ME. Characteristically, he was absorbed in taking pictures with a large digital SLR and paying no attention to Mac or anybody else. Around the victim's wrist were clear signs of restraint: reddening and some adhesive residue. The kid had been bound with duct tape or something similar, and it had then been removed; the right wrist would certainly show the same thing. A quick glance down confirmed what Mac would have already guessed; there were no signs of the feet having been taped up. At some point, this young fellow had been walked or dragged, hands secured, to wherever it was they shot him.

And it was probably going to be 'they'. Having looked deliberately at all the other places he could see, Mac now looked at the back of the kid's head. This was not his favorite thing to do, and for a non-medical investigator, not the most meaningful place to be looking, but it was the crux of it all. As Jenn had said, there were two obvious entry wounds, one above and behind the right ear, and one just off center to the left of the skull, nearly at the top. He'd never seen a truly professional execution before, but this certainly seemed like one; two guys, both with handguns, both shooting the victim in the head at almost the same second. For one thing, it was certain to do the job, and for another, it made it very difficult to prove which shot actually killed him. He understood why Jenn wanted him here.

After another long look around, all around the body, as much as he could see from where he was standing, Mac walked back over to Langton. She was writing notes by hand, trying to keep the paper dry with the flap of her coat.

"This isn't going to be simple," Mac said. "Not killed here, for sure. No blood, practically, for one thing."

"No, no blood at all, really. And they don't seem to have brought anything in with them except the kid himself."

"Nope. And the dual shot thing. That's kind of high-end for what we used to get, that I can recall." Mac was stating the obvious. He'd never seen anything like this, anywhere except in training material, and he knew Langton hadn't either. But the habit of speaking of his experience as being in the past was strong. He wasn't going to assert any kind of current knowledge. "I think his hands were taped."

"Really? I didn't see. Only the left one is sticking out."

"Yeah, it's there. Tape marks. He was tied. Not on the feet, though."

Langton seemed unconcerned that she'd missed that evidence. *Mac's here*, she thought, *he can deal with that. I need to*

18

manage the scene, keep the press away, and sound confident when the chief shows up. And he will. He will. Any minute now.

The press, per se, was actually a nonentity in Ann Arbor. There had been a local newspaper for decades, but they'd closed their doors and gone all-online, firing everybody with any kind of expertise and seniority in the process. Now a bunch of poorly paid or actually unpaid bloggers collected whatever crime news was fed to them and obligingly put it on the net. The Detroit papers, also mostly online, and the Detroit TV stations could be counted on to show up for dramatic moments, but very little in the way of day to day reporting on Ann Arbor appeared. The public was not especially upset, as far as you could tell, by this shortage of responsible journalism. The loudest protests over the demise of the paper had been along the lines of "What about the coupons?!" In this case, the Detroit media would put in an appearance sooner or later, since they could monitor police radio just as well as anybody. That was one of the calls Jenn was waiting to get; the notice that the chief had arrived was the second. The third was not one she was anticipating at all.

The calls came in quick succession. A heads-up from the desk that the Detroit news guys were on the way, and then almost at once, a call from the officer at the parking lot to the effect that the AAPD chief was on the scene.

Chief Fredricks, Pat to just about everybody, was a sort of rare bird: a police administrator not actually loathed by his officers. The union, obviously, didn't have much of a good word for him, since he'd had to implement some deeply unpopular cuts, and one set of the citizenry felt the same way. Another group of taxpayers objected to him loudly and frequently for not cutting farther. Nobody in the downtown business community was happy about his eliminating foot and bike patrols, and there was a tendency on everybody's part to blame every crime that actually did happen on the force's failure to psychically predict and prevent it. None of this was in any way unique to Fredricks; in Michigan's ruinous economy, every city chief and most county sheriff's offices had similar problems with public perception, but for a number of reasons, most of the rank and file cops in Ann Arbor liked and respected their head man. Langton did too, but she was also afraid of him, simply because he was the boss.

She acknowledged the notice of his arrival, and saw Fredricks' car drive out onto the field and turn east toward the scene. At the same time, her cell rang again. It was the chief himself.

"Jenn?" he said, "It's Pat. Be there in a second. You got any idea why the FBI would be here?"

A Forbidding Place

> *Upon this the Gods swear, the primordial, imperishable Water of Styx, and it issues from a forbidding place.*

The FBI, in most matters involving Ann Arbor, meant an old, veteran agent from the Detroit office, Doug Markowitz. Bank robberies, of course, involved the proverbial Feds, at least technically, and there was the occasional odd case; once, after 9/11, some copies of bomb-making information had been found in Afghanistan, still bearing markings that showed their origin: one of Ann Arbor's older businesses, an international microfilm and document search company. Doug got to run that one down, discovering that just about anyone with a library card in most of the semi-civilized world would have had access to them.

Today, Markowitz was back in Ann Arbor, having been rousted out of bed by a phone call on a morning he was supposed to have off. That made him cranky, as did the weather, as did his companion, a new agent just transferred up from Cleveland. There was nothing really wrong with the young man, but anything new was beginning to annoy Doug, especially as retirement approached. Another annoying thing was that Chief Fredricks had driven off out of the parking lot as they pulled in, although Doug knew the chief's car and knew that Fredricks knew his car and knew, also, that he was coming. He could have waited. And he'd been close enough to the chief's vehicle to see that Fredricks had a large cup of coffee, whereas Doug hadn't had a chance to stop for any. *Cranky, petulant ... not unlike a large, gray five-year-old*, he thought. *I better think good thoughts about Ann Arbor before I stick my nose into this little crime scene.*

Although Doug and MacArthur knew each other of old, the Fed missed noticing Mac's pickup in the lot. There was no missing Mac, though, standing with his back to the wind, talking to Fredricks and the woman detective Doug remembered as being a problem, or having been one at one point. If she was the one running things, at least he knew that she'd been gently counseled about local and federal cooperation. But if Mac was in charge, that ran counter to what Doug had heard about his condition and status. Just barging in and yelling, "Who's in charge here?" was not, of course, the right way to conduct business, but there were days, there were days ... especially days like this one.

Andy Patel, the new guy from Cleveland, knew none of this. His call to get out of bed had been even more peremptory than Doug's, and his attempts to find out from Doug what the hell was going on were met with denials of knowledge: "They didn't say. We have to go talk to the local cops," and after another question, "You know, I really don't like to talk and drive at the same time." So Patel didn't know who the little knot of civilian-dressed people were, down at the end of what was apparently an airport runway, in a city he guessed must be Ann Arbor, based on freeway exit signs. It was clearly a crime scene, yellow tape and all, a few uniforms around. But that was about all he had to go on, and it didn't seem as though Markowitz was going to give him anything more.

Of course, the appearance of the FBI agents called for some sort of introduction: "Mac's sort of consulting on this one," Chief Fredricks said. "He's retired."

Doug's large, gray left eyebrow twitched up slightly at that, but he accepted the minor fiction as somehow necessary. Mac and he had always gotten along, although without deep friendship. He acknowledged capability when he found it, and Mac had always been capable – reasonable, too, which was frequently more important. He'd mastered a fair amount of Fed-speak, and that spared Doug from having to explain things, especially things that probably shouldn't be explained too fully to a non-Fed. Today, though, he felt less comfortable with Mac than he remembered being; *there, but for a couple more hamburgers, go I*, was the vaguely unsettling thought. *Will I make it to retirement or won't I?*

Patel, meanwhile, was feeling more and more like a fifth wheel. Nobody had actually introduced anybody, and he could only deduce that the older guy in a dripping wet hat was 'Mac', since the other possibility was a woman. Everybody's badges, if they had badges, were inside clothing, but it seemed unlikely that these three people would be down here at the scene if they weren't cops. Since Markowitz had mentioned the locals, these must be the locals.

"So, Pat," the senior agent was saying, "We don't know dick about your case. I just got a call to grab this guy – Andy Patel, by the way, this is Chief Fredricks – and get out here. Maybe because of the airport, maybe just because I was supposed to be off today. Whadda ya got, if you don't mind saying?"

"I wouldn't mind at all," said Fredricks, "if I knew dick myself. Just got here. It's a black kid, shot in the head from behind and dumped. Beyond that, I'm waiting on Ansel Adams over there to finish his photo shoot."

"So it didn't happen here?"

"No, not enough blood, no empties, some drag marks. Looks like he was shot someplace else and brought here."

"No ID yet?"

"Nope. Once digital boy actually rolls him over and lets us look in his pockets we might have one – I kind of doubt it, though."

Doug thought that over for a second. He was bare-headed, and the rain was vastly annoying, cold and trickling down the back of his coat collar, splashing on his glasses. He envied Mac his hat.

"You know," he said, "maybe we could find someplace back at the parking lot to camp out. Is there a lobby or something?"

"I think there's a meeting room or a class room or something like that," Mac said. "I think I was at a conference once in there."

"I'll check," Langton said, speaking up for the first time. If she could get the Feds and maybe even the chief out of her hair, she'd feel better. She didn't believe for a minute that Markowitz 'didn't know dick' about the case. He knew something she didn't, something the chief didn't. Probably Mac didn't know, either. The absolute best thing in the next hour would be for the FBI and Chief Fredricks to hole up in a nice dry conference room somewhere and leave the detectives alone. It didn't work out that way.

"Doug," said Mac, "how about if you and I and ... Andy, is it? ... Go back up there and see what we can occupy. Leave Langton and the chief down here to work through the ID, if there is one, get the scene squared away. For one thing, they've only got two runways here, and they're going to want this one back, sooner or later." It was stating the obvious, but it accomplished any number of things. It told Langton that she was going to have to step up and do the leg work, it gave Doug and his companion an excuse to get out of the rain and not contribute any more cooks to the kitchen than necessary, and it got him, Mac, out of the damn rain and cold, too. If there were going to be Feds in on this thing, he'd end up talking to them, and the ideal environment for that would be a controlled, comfortable space, with coffee, preferably.

In fact, there was a conference room, paneled like a north woods bar and with an equally rustic plaque, whose router-lettering read, 'Inch by inch, anything's a cinch'. Mac remembered it from a community gathering or maybe some kind of liaison with Township cops about some burning issue – football traffic, probably. They assorted themselves around a folding table, and silently pondered the lack of amenities; there was no obvious coffee. Doug wondered if Andy was junior enough to be sent out for some and decided that he was probably not. Mac had finished his and was wishing he had another, more for something to do than for the caffeine. Cops were supposed to know things, and the state of knowing nothing useful was uncomfortable for everybody. Patel was doubly uncomfortable for a wider range of reasons, but it was just a matter of scope. An uneasy silence descended.

Markowitz caved in first. "So, like I said, they didn't tell me why to get out here, but maybe I can do a little guessing." Mac nodded slightly and made an 'I'm listening' face.

"Right now, the Agency is really twitchy about anything unusual that even smells like coke …" Doug let that one sit in the air for a minute. "I guess I should say, everybody is, not just the Agency, but all the Agencies."

"More so than usual?" Mac asked.

"Yeah, I'd say more so. Maybe a lot more so."

"Nothing about this smells like anything yet," Mac pointed out, "Unless there's a sniff I'm not getting."

"I know," said Doug, "Nothing for me, either, except a very public murder, young black kid, all that."

"And you were supposed to be off-duty today, too. Not like you were doing anything useful."

Doug let that go. A number of remarks about not doing useful things with one's time came to mind, but they all ran up against the word 'cancer', and he couldn't think of any way around it.

"Patel, you want to go get the laptop?" Doug asked. "Maybe we can take some notes when there's anything to take notes about." This was a fair example of the general utility that Andy got to exhibit when working with Markowitz, and he was almost used to it. Fetch and carry.

"Sure. You have the keys." Doug slid them across the table, and Andy went out, zipping up his coat as he went.

"He's a hungry little prick," Doug said, after the door was closed. "Wants to know a lot more than he needs to on everything. Cleveland got tired of it and gave him to us."

"Well, I sympathize in this particular scenario," said Mac. "I'd like to know something about it, myself. Right now, I wouldn't even go on paper about the kid's gender."

"Looked like a guy."

"Yeah. Never been fooled by appearances, though?"

"Not at close range, anyway."

This light badinage was interrupted by the door; Andy came back in, carrying a shoulder bag, and followed immediately by one of the uniformed cops from down at the end of the runway. "This officer's looking for you, Mr. MacArthur," he said. "Says they've got an ID already."

"Sheriff's Department passed along a missing person report," said the officer. "Parents called in when he wasn't in his bedroom this morning. Rodney James Garfield, twenty-two years old, lived with his parents at," – he looked at a page from a notebook – "222 Oakwood, Rome."

At the word Rome, Doug's left eyebrow twitched again. Mac had been watching Markowitz, and he caught the giveaway. The Fed's interest was not just coke, but coke and Rome and maybe Metro Airport and maybe a murder that had some professional-sounding aspects.

Oak Tree or Stone

But why all this about oak tree or stone?

Over the next few hours, the various agencies involved learned a great deal about Rodney James Garfield. Appearances at the crime scene had been proven out: he was in fact a male, of African-American descent. He was born in 1990 to a single mother; she subsequently married a man who was either Rodney's birth father or believed he was. Rodney went to school through the tenth grade in a large, consolidated suburban district, before fading away from attendance. He had no drivers' license – he was one of those people the police contact frequently who carry no ID at all. He had of course, been arrested for driving without said license and twice more for possession of small amounts of marijuana. Most recently and slightly more interestingly, he'd been sentenced for fleeing and eluding police and resisting arrest with violence. For that, he'd been incarcerated in one of Wayne County's large jails, and his face still showed the marks of a beating he'd allegedly taken from another inmate. He'd been released just a week ago, on parole, and was not supposed to be out of his parents' house between six PM and eight AM. His presence at the end of runway six with two gunshot wounds in the back of his head suggested that he'd violated the terms of his parole sometime in the last twenty-four hours.

None of this added up to a drug cartel war. Not to speak ill of the dead, Rodney was an insignificant petty criminal. If he'd been shot in the chest at twenty feet by unknown persons driving by in a stolen car, or fatally stabbed in a dispute over forty dollars' worth of weed, or killed in a collision while running from a traffic stop, nobody would have gotten very excited. When his body was searched, there was literally nothing to connect him to the drug trade: no contraband, no paraphernalia, no list of names in Spanish with quantities in kilograms delivered by date and address – nothing except that he was from Rome and had been very carefully extinguished in a way that couldn't help but be publicly noticed.

But for both of those reasons, he was a problem. He was dead in Ann Arbor, and that made him Ann Arbor's problem. If the actual place where he'd been shot turned out to be somewhere else, it just brought another agency into the mix. The Rome connection made him the concern of any number of federal offices, right now all concentrated in the person of Doug Markowitz. And all those years of being professionally curious, coupled with a desire not to be completely sidelined, meant that this would keep Mac up at night, too. Eventually, he'd know something about the boy, eventually Mac would have a mental model of Rodney's last night. It would be substantially wrong, but he'd have one. Before that, though, he'd have to go through the fire, a fire started years before, lit by a man now dead.

They had over-reached themselves

> *But great Ouranos used to call the sons he begot*
> *Titans, a reproachful nickname, because he thought*
> *They had over-reached themselves and done a*
> *monstrous deed*

For which vengeance later would surely be exacted.

Western Michigan is a different place in some ways than the southeastern three-quarter circle that includes and surrounds Detroit. The minority population is a smaller percentage of the whole, and the real underclass of unemployed and reckless young men is whiter than it is in the East Coast cities. Muskegon and Benton Harbor are sketchy, dangerous mid-size towns, but Grand Rapids is by reputation of Dutch background, slightly better off, and not quite as affected by Midwest decay as Detroit, Flint, Saginaw, and Pontiac. Nevertheless, it's got some edgy suburbs, and the close-in satellite town of Montana, Michigan, certainly ranks among them.

Nine years before Rodney Garfield showed up at the Ann Arbor airport, a man named Clay DeVoos was trying to build a small entrepreneurship in and around Montana, playing a couple of separate but related games: rural real estate speculation and the fundamental Christianity biz. Sundays, Clay gathered a few followers in a frame building, out in the countryside, sitting on a two-acre lot he'd leased. At the church, Clay preached a sort of nasty sub-Baptist gospel, with a lot more pro-forma singing and praying than philosophical discourse. The people who were attracted to Clay's sermons weren't really critical thinkers. They tended to be needy in some way, some of them financially needy, and with many added variations of illness, alienation, loneliness, advancing age, resentment of their damn ungrateful children, and simple ignorance. It wasn't a joyous church, but it filled some purpose for the congregation, since they kept coming back. They put a few dollars in the collection plate, came to the very occasional evening events, and talked a lot of farm-country gossip. None of it paid even the rent on the church, let alone any kind of salary for Clay. But some of the parishioners were owners of farm land, one, two, or three hundred acre holdings, out past the suburban towns. Knowing about and gaining the trust of these older people was DeVoos' only reason for having started the church.

Clay was born in the late Thirties, and he was too young for the Second World War and Korea. He skated by Vietnam and so missed the big wars. He got a simple degree from Western Michigan University – English or anthropology or something like that – and tried his hand at the family business. That might have worked out, but he couldn't keep his mind on furniture and off the cash that went through the shop. After he'd found three or four creative ways to slide small percentages of the revenue into his own pocket, his relatives figured out what must be going on. There was a quiet little family meeting, first without Clay and then with him, and it ended with an agreement: Clay would take a small loan from the company and get into real estate. Everybody would keep their opinions and hurt feelings to themselves, and Clay would not look back or ask for anything else. Afterward, Clay could recall a sense of getting off easy, a lessening of his respect for the family elders, and the unreality of family events. Thanksgiving, Christmas, wakes and weddings, all went on with the same white-bread blandness they always had. He'd had a plan which had not been carefully thought through, perhaps, but it wasn't his fault; he was structurally incapable of admitting that it was his fault. It had fallen apart on him, and now he had to find a new way of making a living.

He wasn't without a level of intelligence, and the real estate boards had admitted far bigger idiots than Clay. He studied and passed, and he got set up with a medium-size, regional agency. His book of business was mostly existing homes in lower-income areas in and around the town of Montana. He tried commercial real estate for a while, but the problem there was that both sides in the transaction tended to be pros; the property owners with space to lease were on top of their game – had to be – and the buyers, the people who leased storefronts and offices and shopping center pads, were businessmen, sometimes businessmen representing very large, very well lawyered-up companies. The opportunities to run a fast one of any kind were few.

In residential property, on the other hand, the buyer was almost always an amateur. How many houses did one family buy, after all? And the more they thought they knew, the better, since it was easier to honey up to them, one expert to another. A little knowledge, if you were dealing with Clay, was more dangerous than having none. And in Clay's business, the residential sellers were usually individuals, too. He tried to keep it that way. It made either side of the equation, representing buyer *or* seller, a much more attractive proposition for a conscienceless borderline sociopath to profit from. So, he stayed with the family-level deals and stayed clear of the developer market.

Clay spent the next thirty years of his life squeezing whatever he could out of these older home sales. Along the way, his mother introduced him to a girl from church, and to foster the family's 'Clay has straightened out' myth, he married her. She was wrapped as tightly as he was, as it turned out, given to vague fears and depressions and with an overbearing mother of her own on whose advice she relied. She had a 'business' associate's degree, and she could type and keep books. She made Clay a nice little unpaid employee.

It wasn't much of a marriage beyond that. Sex and children and anything but the most superficial bows to social respectability were not part of Clay's psychological makeup. He avoided golf, for example, although almost all his colleagues paid lip service to it. He went to church to avoid difficulties with his wife, but there was nothing else in his life that would have given you an impression of faith. He got his leads through the agencies – several of them, over the years – with whom he operated, and paid almost no attention to word of mouth or networking. His best, most profitable buyers and sellers weren't people he wanted to meet socially. They probably thought the same of him.

Along the way, Clay and his wife produced exactly one child, a son, Eugene. The boy grew up in the sensory-deprived world of his father and his nine-to-five deals and his nights in front of the TV, and Eugene eventually learned to do some of the leg work and make some of the repairs that Clay conned sellers into making. By the time he was out of high school, father and son were talking about the advantages of Eugene getting a contractor's license and setting up a separate company, just to make the conflicts of interest less obvious.

By then, though, it was the Nineties, and the boom in new housing was ballooning up. Turning cornfields into McMansions was the new gold rush. The market for existing homes was tapering off, and almost anyone with a pulse could get a mortgage for three, four, or five hundred thousand dollars on a jerry-built, garish pile twenty or thirty miles out from the urban limits. Lots of agents chased those six-figure sales, but Clay sat down and figured out his odds. They weren't good. Too many people were running around with big-agency signs on their SUVs, building offices for themselves, for God's sake – his had always been his kitchen table and his car. He needed a way to keep on tapping an uneducated side of the equation without spending anything on upgrading his image or facilities or risk. That ruled out the developers as clients – they were plenty educated, if sometimes a bit wild-eyed in their planning. Where was the common man, the guy who knew little or nothing about real estate, easily intimidated by a well-spoken white guy in a suit, the man, not to put too fine a point on it, who Clay could bamboozle? The answer seemed simple enough: it was the elderly farmers who actually owned hundred-acre cornfields.

On the days when he didn't have anything on his calendar –
and they were increasing – he started driving around in the
country, looking at the developments, noting the locations, and
looking up the transactions in which the developer got his
hands on the land. Frequently, the property had passed quickly
from corporation to corporation in the previous twelve
months, but with few exceptions, the people at the back of it
were Mr. and Mrs. Old-resident, who'd owned the property
since they inherited it from one or the other of their parents,
forty or fifty years back. Two or three years before the
bulldozers came in, these old folks would have sold the whole
parcel or at least a big piece of it to a company, and usually
they'd gotten a large amount of money (by the standard of
Clay's usual deals). That amount would be far less than the sum
of the prices of the houses to be built on it, but still huge –
seven figures. To get to a point where you could recoup that
kind of investment, you had to have capitalization, employees,
equipment; you had to be in an actual business. But just to get
a piece of the initial transaction price, Clay figured you didn't
have to have much more than he already had: a kitchen table,
a realtor's license, and a persistence with obstacles, human and
official. He hadn't made many strategic business decisions in
his life, but this time, he saw one looking back at him from the
notes on his legal pad. He couldn't afford to sit back and slowly
go out of business. He decided to bet the farm.

Ah, but the primary obstacle was: he didn't know any of those
old folks. He knew a few other realtors, his supervisors and
contacts in the agencies, title company drones, some lawyers,
barbers, convenience store employees, the salesmen at a car
dealership. But rural people? Farmers? No, got none of them in
the Rolodex. He thought about it for a few more days, still
driving around out in the county, and it came to him somehow
that part of the respect he'd lost for his own family had
centered on their faith. They'd let him slide because they
heard, every Sunday, that man is fundamentally good, and that

malfeasance is the work of Satan, not the simple act of one person taking advantage of another. He suspected, in fact, that the family minister had been consulted, before the brothers let him slide out of what had been frank and simple larceny. Although his lip twitched slightly every time he thought about it, just a hint of a sneer breaking through his pasty expression, it gave him an idea. People go to church to gossip, to stave off loneliness, and to listen for an hour or so to someone who had asserted a right to their trust. What would it take to tap into that, out there in the rural neighborhoods, find out who was getting past their prime and maybe looking to cash in, and get them to give Clay a piece of the deal? What would it take, in fact, to start his own church?

After another week of his pedestrian but extremely thorough research methods, the answer was on another page of a yellow pad. You did not, in fact, have to have any actual training or ordination or credentials. Especially if you steered well clear of claiming tax exempt status (and making money from the church was no part of the plan at all), nobody official would give a damn about it. You could call yourself the Reverend DeVoos, come up with a credible backstory to explain the lack of big-church affiliation, and just go for it. His wife was a capable enough secretary to help with the minimal record keeping, his son could be a general handyman and an example of pious and obedient youth, and somehow he, Clay, would brush up enough on at least the New Testament to crank out a weekly sermon. Trust would be a big part of the message. And although it would never, never come up during services, it wouldn't be long before the people in the audience — excuse me, the congregation — would come to know that Clay was also a trustworthy ally in any dealings with developers, lawyers, and so on. Imagine: their very own minister, also a skilled and upright realtor. And that nice Eugene boy, just starting out as a contractor. What a coincidence. How reassuring.

On the down side, he'd have to take the cost of a church building somewhere out there off the side of his real estate practice. Not in his wildest assumptions was there any possibility of getting enough in the collection plate for that. Further, it would be a certain amount of work, of a kind he'd never done, to be a public figure and stand up to speak once a week. And of course, he had to explain it, probably in two different levels of detail, to his wife and son. The rest of the family could go merrily to hell, but he needed the wife and the boy to make it work.

The Nemean Lion

> *... the Nemean lion that Zeus' dutiful wife*
> *Hera raised to roam and ravage Nemea's hills*
> *A spectral killer that destroyed whole villages,*
> *Master of Nemean Tretos and Apesas.*
> *But Herekles muscled him down in the end.*

Clay thought it all through for another day, then sat down with Eugene in the evening, after Mom had gone to bed. He started it out logically, moving from the decline in their traditional business. He called it 'their' business deliberately and for the first time. He touched on the easy state of credit, meaning that people with anything like actual money would be buying new homes, not existing ones, and he linked that to an inevitable decline in the side business, Eugene's handyman work. From there, he moved quickly on to the solution (he was afraid that otherwise the boy would think it was a prelude to asking him to move out of the house), the notion of getting into the brokerage business, out in the farm land. He walked through the basic economics of these acreage deals, making it clear that there'd be a big investment of time in each one, but a big payoff too, much bigger than anything they'd been seeing. He made what to a nineteen-year-old high school grad would have sounded like a clear cut case for the deal. And then he brought up the problem.

"Problem is," Clay said, "We don't know any of those people. Can't just walk up and knock on the door and say, 'How'd you like to sell your land?' They have to trust us. And that's where my idea gets a bit unusual."

It was actually somewhat surprising, Clay thought later on, how easily the boy had bought into it. He'd been caught off guard, but he saw the point. Eugene hadn't been attending any form of religious service for years. Clay only went out of habit and to placate his wife. The boy had no theological objections to forming a splinter sect. He was mildly concerned that there were no ministerial credentials in the family, but Clay covered that easily enough, taking it all on himself. All Gene would have to do is be the dutiful son and, by the way, president of his own contracting company. He, Clay, would deal with the doctrinal aspects. The president thing was a new one, something Clay had thought up fast, just an hour or so before, as an added inducement, and it worked. If Gene had any kind of role model within the nuclear family, it was self-employment, being one's own boss. He hadn't especially enjoyed his experiences with being an employee, so far: a couple of convenience store jobs and things like that. If the price was to act as fixit man and spear carrier for his father's new church, that price could be paid. And so, also for the first time, they shook hands on it. Now for Mom.

Clay brought it up at breakfast, and predictably, she was not as easy a sell. First of all, it would mean going to two services. That was her primary objection: she would, of course, keep on going to her regular church. That was obvious. But she'd have to show up at Clay's services, too. How would that work? They'd have to have two cars, for heaven's sake. And what about choir practice? This sort of thing went on for an hour or so, with Clay delivering answers he'd thought of before or

35

coming up with workarounds for the issues he hadn't foreseen. But he had a trump card, like the contracting company idea for Eugene. At the wife's current place of worship, she was rank and file. At his church, she could run things. Choir practice, for example. She could build up a choir of her own, if she wanted to.

After they'd been at it for a while, Clay realized with a mild shock that the topic he'd been dreading, the blunt, hard to answer question, 'Why?' hadn't come up. Somehow, his announcement that he was thinking of starting his own church had not triggered any but detail objections. Nor had she called into question the overall wisdom of the venture. It came to him that over all these years he'd been missing something about the woman: she trusted him and thought he was capable. In other words, she was not just a bit of a dull crayon, she was actually not all there — a taco shy of a combo meal, as he'd heard some kid say. This was a new factor; it'd honestly never occurred to him, and he'd have to keep it in mind. The seedier aspects of his current real estate dealings weren't necessarily apparent to his wife, since she acted just as a bookkeeper and calendar manager, and he kept both of those repositories scrupulously clean, but with this new thing ... well, he'd have to be careful with her, that's all. More careful than he'd planned on.

Eventually, as he hoped it would, cupidity won out. He dangled the chance to be somebody, in a hopelessly trivial sense of that phrase, well enough that she agreed. She never asked him what he planned on preaching or what kind of vocation had come to him, late in middle age. She never questioned the financial aspects of it; Clay slowly grasped the fact that he might just as well have said he was opening a restaurant or a hardware store. She apparently thought that you did things like that, and you charged people money, and you kept on eating and having a roof overhead. Her view of the economy and the real estate business and so on was no more sophisticated than her view of God and the hereafter. There were only details, only minor annoyances to be overcome, never any real question of success or failure. He wondered, briefly, what she thought happened to the impoverished, elderly, often minority people whose houses he listed and sold and whose savings he channeled to repair contractors (and to Eugene). Did it occur to her that they might have had some expectation of succeeding in life, of affording something more than a room in a cheap nursing home? Apparently not. If he had actually been a theologian, the word 'predestination' might have come to mind, but he wasn't, and neither was his wife.

It took a while, three months to be precise, to gather up the threads of the project. Clay was resigned to just about any structure for the church that was usable, but he lucked onto a find: a one-story building that had in fact been a church, with a dirt parking lot already in place, and a pole barn out back that would be a great headquarters for Eugene DeVoos Services, Inc. Some kind of fundamentalist creed had built the place, back in the Seventies, and gone castors up due to the mistaken assumption that it would pay for itself. It sat on two acres, and Clay was able (like so many, many dubious people at the time) to get financing. At the last minute, though, he thought better of buying it outright, and convinced the bank that owned the site to go for a month to month lease instead. Having seen no revenue at all from it for years, the bank agreed, and the DeVoos family began cleaning and clearing up and advertising their plans. In a short period of time, most of the farm families within thirty miles knew that somebody was going to start up a church. Not long after that, they knew that it would be called the Farmer's First Community Church, and people split down the middle on how that name was meant; was it the first such church, or was it the church that put farmers first? Either way, it was a curiosity, and forty-some people showed up on the first Sunday it was open.

Two months later, there weren't quite so many, but the demographics had sorted themselves out pretty much as Clay expected they would. There were exactly two young families, neither of them owning any land at all; five or six single congregants, most of whom seemed to see it as a dating opportunity; and four of the actual target group, two older couples who were still sitting on their family farms and getting pestered by developers. These were the people Clay chatted with after services, after his wife's half-witted attempts at choir practice, after the usual polite exchanges among people just getting to know each other. These were the folks who discovered, very casually, that Clay's son was good with a hammer. And not too long after that, it came up that what Clay did during the week was real estate; had been doing it for decades. Knew everybody in the business, in fact, clear on into Grand Rapids. They came to know, too, that he was supporting the church out of his own pocket.

And that was when things went off the rails. It had never been part of Clay's thinking that he would be anything more than a broker between the old folks and the money men. He'd assumed that if he got his foot in the door with the landowners, he'd be the one the McMansion boys would have to talk to. What he hadn't counted on was their being smarter than that.

The Currys, the one family that was actually talking to anyone about selling, agreed to have Clay step in. He almost promised them that, without help, they were going to be screwed out of the full value of their place, and the Currys let him take over. But when he announced himself to the developers as the seller's agent and handed them a counter price, they slammed the door in his face. They told him in no uncertain terms that they'd deal with owners or nobody, and he could take his realtor's license and insert it in any orifice he chose as long as it was one of his own.

Clay, as we've already noted, was not used to having extremes of emotion, and the cold fury he now felt made him physically ill. The reaction was compounded of one part wounded pride and an equal part guilt at having overlooked such an obvious flaw in his plan. He remembered how it had felt to be caught with his hand in the till, back at the furniture store. Hovering around in his psyche was a carefully hidden and repressed component of self-doubt and self-loathing, but it was not anything he ever let come to the surface. Anything at all was preferable to letting that demon out of its cage. This was not — not! — his fault!

Usually, when the cause of a setback was something trivial, Clay could enjoy the luxury of a slow, revenge-is-a-dish-best-eaten-cold reaction, and if the revenge never happened, time and the pleasure of imagining it repeatedly would take the edge off. Every single one of the three or four traffic tickets he'd had in his life had been examples. Damn cops, bothering him, a local businessman, who dedicated his life to helping people with their real estate problems, when there were real criminals out there. He'd undergo twenty-four hours of brooding anger, devising ways of getting back at officialdom, visualizing some way of screwing the officer over in a home sale, getting him to pay more or sell for less than was wise. None of those things ever came to pass, because he never got the chance to buy or sell a house for any cop, let alone one who'd written him a ticket. And the sheer pleasure of replaying the conversation, pretending to himself that he'd made cutting insinuations about the policeman's ability, tenure in the job, and vulnerability to civil action, would take the sting out of these affronts. Usually a day or so after he'd paid the fine, he'd move on.

But this! Those miserable bastards! They wouldn't even talk to him, let alone help him with his plan to become the farm-sale king of the county. After all the work he'd put into the church, all the careful talk, coming up with those damn sermons every week, being so, so cautious not to offend anyone, right, left, or otherwise! And below it was a mocking voice that said, "They'll all do it. One group has your name now. It'll get around. Watch out for the preacher-realtor, they'll tell each other. You should have guessed, you should have known, you should have foreseen ...." When the voice, which was his conscience if he'd been willing to admit it, reached that point, he'd bang the steering wheel and try frantically to imagine his next move.

Of course, he didn't say anything to his wife and son, nor to the landowners, Jack and Jeanne Curry. He drove around aimlessly for an hour, quartering back and forth across the county, and slowly his anger morphed into its typical second phase, from "They can't treat me that way," to "All right, if that's how you want it." If the money boys wouldn't deal with anyone but landowners, all right, by God, Clay would be a landowner. It was a childish reaction, born of having his essentially childish scheme blow up in his face, but he thought maybe it might not be such a wild notion.

The Curry farm was three hundred and sixty acres in all. Nobody, not even the banks of that long gone age, would loan Clay DeVoos the money for all of that. But what if he could get the Currys to sell him a strategic piece of it? What if he could get a loan that would make the developer come to him, hat in hand, if they didn't want a nice big, say, twenty acre, gap in their happy subdivision? Now he was actually starting to hyperventilate a bit. What if that gap were going to be used for a landfill or a junkyard? Or a pig farm? He wouldn't actually have to do any such thing, just let it be known that he intended to. Land was land, ownership was a matter of who got the funding and the deal. And he had a relationship with more than one banker, after all.

He slowly calmed down and began thinking it through. He sifted the various bankers of his acquaintance and came up with one high enough in his bank to approve such a loan but not high enough to see a corporate opportunity and undercut Clay with the sellers. He estimated how long he could make payments on the purchase and how much longer after that he could stall while he waited to sell his parcel. And somehow, he failed to see the trap there, failed to see that all a bigger operation had to do was out-wait him. Or maybe he did see it and glossed it over; it was not a decision he discussed with anybody.

It took another three weeks, but he talked the Currys into giving him an option on eighteen acres of their farm, right in the middle of the tract and with road access. He told them that it was a lever for moving the developer up a notch in the offering price. He convinced his banker that there was money to be made, based on inside knowledge of a pending sale, and he got his funding ducks in a row, proposing to put his house up as collateral. Then, he sat back and waited. It took just about another week.

The developers thought they'd seen the last of Clay, and after letting the Currys steep for a good long time, they showed back up on a Sunday morning with a slightly higher offer. Their hope was that they'd been sufficiently arrogant and unpleasant to drive off that preacher, and that the Currys would now be willing to talk reasonably. The new offer was still half a million dollars less than they were actually prepared to pay, but it was a nice, round six-figure number more than their opening bid.

Naturally, since Clay had said nothing truthful to them about his experience with McMansions Inc., the Currys thought he'd accomplished this price jump for them, and they were inclined to accept. Then it occurred to Mrs. Curry to bring up the topic of Clay's option. The Alpha lawyer in the room looked it over quickly and then a second time. There was a long pause, after which all offers were withdrawn, the briefcases packed up, and the legal boys and girls drove away in their rented Lexus. There were phone calls and unhappiness, and Clay ended up driving out to confer with the Currys.

Misty Tartaros

> *... they sent them under*
> *the wide-pathed earth and bound them with cruel*
> *bonds*
> *Having beaten them down despite their daring*
> *As far under earth as the sky is above*
> *For it is that far from earth down to misty Tartaros.*

Jack Curry had spent 1965 and most of 1966 in the Republic of Vietnam, serving with the US Fifth Cavalry. He'd taken part in the dismal fighting in the Ia Drang valley, seen the confusion and command incompetence on both sides, flaws that were not compensated for by the individual courage of the men doing the shooting. When he got home, he got out. For a long time, he was withdrawn and nationalistic about it all, but watching the 1975 evacuation on television got him over a lot of that. He never felt the resentment that some vets did for the idea that the US 'lost' in Vietnam. Instead, he came around to a sweeping condemnation of all the leadership of that period. It was a kind of white, lower-class agrarian version of "Charlie never called me ..." He felt no anger at the Vietnamese, except for the idiotic southern government. He wore out his welcome at the VFW hall by saying publicly that a veteran of that war was a veteran, no matter what side he'd been on. He refused to visit the Wall because it had only American names on it. He never threw his medals over the White House fence because he didn't have any to throw, and it wouldn't have occurred to him, anyway. He'd fought in a war, probably killed some people (no way of knowing, really), and it had made him a sort of conditional pacifist. America's participation in the Second World War he accepted as necessary; beyond that, he couldn't see any justification for fighting at all.

This didn't make him a very popular guy with other vets or politicians or those of a conservative or Fourth-of-July-patriot bent. Until he learned to keep his mouth shut about it all, except in company with people whose opinions he already knew, it cost him friends. But it did get him a wife, a pretty, cheerful daughter of a Quaker family, themselves already at odds with the West Michigan point of view. Jeanne was the only daughter, the only child, of a farmer who owned a large dairy and corn farm, out in the county. Jack was looking around for something more than a bitter agnosticism, and when he sampled a bit of the small Quaker congregation's activities, he wasn't all that impressed with the doctrine, but he fell quietly and extensively in love with Jeanne.

Fortunately, her parents liked Jack. They liked his good manners and his political credo, such as it was. Although he wasn't an especially literary guy, and writing down what he thought about things was not a habit, his courting letters to Jeanne (yes, although they lived twelve miles apart, they wrote letters to each other) were open and honest and completely believable. Jeanne used to read selected passages to her mother, and eyes weren't always dry afterward.

Jack and Jeanne married in 1979, and he split his time helping with his own parents' farm and hers. But when Jeanne's father passed on and then, shortly after, her mother, the kids inherited the land. Jeanne had grown up on it, and Jack came to regard it as home almost at once. His own father, still living and working the land in defiance of all actuarial data, needed help, but on that side there were brothers and a sister to pitch in, and Jack focused on what he still called 'Jeanne's place'. He farmed it, using what he knew from his own upbringing and what he'd learned from Jeanne's parents. He did well, as well as independent farmers ever do.

Over the years, the Currys had two children, both of whom were now out of the house and out of Michigan, too. One of them had already come up with the obligatory grandchild. As Jack and Jeanne finished out their fifties and began to get used to the idea of becoming sixty-something, neither was really discontented, but perhaps just a bit bored with agriculture and living a long way from anything more developed than a convenience store. Retirement on money from cashing in the farm seemed like something to think about, and setting aside college money for the grandchildren, too. Yes, there was just the one so far, but both Jack's and Jeanne's families were prolific. There was every reason to assume there'd be more.

Unfortunately, though, there was a bad hand waiting to be dealt, and it had nothing to do with real estate or Clay DeVoos or housing bubbles. What no one, Jack included, knew about Jack was that he was beginning to suffer from dementia. Plaque of a certain kind was forming in his brain, and it was making him, imperceptibly, lose his grip on daily, physical reality. It was slow, very slow, so slow that he saw only the effects, not the pattern. Because those effects (he didn't think of them as 'symptoms') were embarrassing, he hid them as best he could, and he did it well. He kept spare keys to the house and the cars, so that when he lost a set, he'd have more. He learned to play out a story or anecdote in his mind first, before speaking it, to be sure he hadn't forgotten the name of some uncle or acquaintance. It hadn't gotten to the point where he'd forget roads and directions and things, as long as it was close to home. But he did often slip off into a kind of dreaming state, and catch himself just short of talking out loud to people dead for years, some of them dead since 1965, in fact. Jeanne, who was full of plans for what they'd do after they sold the farm, wasn't paying much attention. When she did see something indicative, she'd just think Jack was getting old, that's all. So was she. Time for both of them to retire and go live nearer the grandchildren.

And that was a handle for Jack. He kept his eye on that goal: sell the place and have a load of money to make the old lady happy. It was something to focus on, that and a growing fondness for walking around the land, looking hard at it and trying to commit it to memory, before it was all sold and paved over. Jeanne was a most humane and non-predatory sort, and she paid no more attention to things like hunting seasons than she did to Jack's ever-clearer symptoms. She didn't consider it remarkable when he started carrying his old thirty-thirty deer rifle on these walks, especially since he never shot anything.

Jack was off on one of those walks as Clay drove out to the house to talk. He'd left Eugene to deal with the Sunday services, the first time he'd done that, but the boy had the sermon to read, and he knew the rest of the drill well enough. Between the two of them, they understood what the priority project was, and all Clay had had to say was that he was going out to talk with the Currys. Gene understood.

Clay DeVoos was used to unpleasant chats with clients, convincing people that their house probably wouldn't sell for the hundred and fifty thousand they wanted, convincing them that a hundred and five was as good an offer as they'd get, getting them to sell before he used up any more of his time on them for the percentage he got out of it. His cut of a hundred and five wasn't all that much less than what he'd get for their asking price, and the longer it took to get a buyer, the more money it cost Clay, in his time and in other small ways. And so he was used to coming up with a set of options or talking points on the way to meetings. But this time, it was for far bigger stakes and a much bigger downside. If the Currys didn't sell or just wanted him to step out, all the effort and the money (and there had been some money he'd had to spend, for sure), on the church had been a waste. He could go on with it, but the Currys had been plain luck, the coincidental timing of their deal and his getting to know them was, as he now saw it, almost too good to be real, and he couldn't see another such coming along soon.

And so he listed his options as essentially three paths, three things he could influence or try to make happen. *One*, he could take the noble-preacher high ground and just step aside. No win for Clay on that one, except that it might help with some other seller, sometime in the future. If the Currys talked about him as being big about it all and giving up his option on the land, that might do him some good, somewhere down the road. But it was all goodwill, nothing you could bank, nothing you could leverage to something bigger.

Two, he could come up with a number, something less than the total increase from the first developer offer to the second, and make a case that his efforts on the Currys' behalf were worth that amount. He could claim and maybe get away with claiming that his option had somehow worked some magic and gotten the price raised, and therefore he'd actually helped them out, just as he said he could. It might sound thin, but still, the second offer was a reasonable amount higher than the first offer had been, and the only difference, as far as the Currys knew, was that Clay had been involved. So now he could propose dropping the option in order to let the deal go forward, and suggest that the Currys pay him for it off the record. Kind of an unofficial commission for getting them more money in total. It would take a while to collect, and it wouldn't be anything like the big payday he'd had in mind, but it would at least be revenue, something to offset the church expenses, and show Eugene and the wife that they were on some kind of a road to black ink.

Or *three*, he could put on a righteous face and denounce the developers as unprofessional, unscrupulous, and untrustworthy. He could suggest that there wasn't all that much expertise needed in what they planned to do. What's building a few houses, after all? Why don't you and I — yes, you, Jack and Jeanne and I — incorporate and develop the farm ourselves?

That thought stopped him cold for a minute. He'd rejected out of hand the notion of going it alone, since he had nothing he could use for money. But the Currys owned the land already. They didn't need a mortgage to buy three hundred and sixty acres; they already had three hundred and sixty acres. And that land could become the collateral for the rest of what they'd need: building a model house or two, getting surveys done, grading streets. Power and water and sewer, those were all things Clay didn't really know much about, except that you had to have 'em. But some of that was on the municipality, right? Not the streets, probably. But a lot of the infrastructure would be on the taxpayers, wouldn't it? His chest felt tight, and his breathing was quicker with the thought of it. Tons of work, tons of things to find out, but with partners who already owned the key asset, hell, maybe it could work.

Or, he thought. Or it could work for a while, anyway, and during that time, Clay could figure out something else, a variation on the theme, something that being one half of a development company with a big chunk of land on the asset side of the ledger would make possible. And what he had to do was convince two aging farmers that the intellectual assets he brought to the deal would be an equivalent contribution. It was a stunning notion. It opened things up. The problem with the current developer faded to insignificance alongside the new challenges.

As he made the last turn toward the Curry farm, option one was already crossed off his list. He wasn't going to walk away from something he'd worked hard to create. Option two became small and despicable and unworthy of his deal-making skills. Option three, Clay the developer, the user of other people's money, became more and more the goal. By the time he was turning into the driveway, he'd made up his mind.

A Forgetting of Troubles

They were born on Pieria after our Father Kronion
Mingled with Memory, who rules Eleutherae's hills.
She bore them to be a forgetting of troubles,
A pause in sorrow ...

In Michigan when winter breaks and the temperature starts getting up to fifty degrees, the land begins to show its proliferation of growth again. Snow hides the fact that a temperate climate is almost as productive as a tropical one when it comes to plant life. Every square inch that isn't paved or plowed or maintained as a lawn grows some kind of wild plant, and those things remain over winter, even if they're dead. Goldenrod dies off, above the ground, but the stems and the spearhead leaves dry to a khaki color with darker brown elongated spots. Berry bushes emerge from the snow as looping tangles of dark red thorny stems.

On paths and in wet patches and places where the previous year hasn't managed to grow tall plants, green grasses start to poke up; in other places, the green is moss, especially if the winter was wetter than it was cold. Long before deciduous trees start to bud, small yellow and blue wild flowers poke out of the ground, and the Redwing Blackbird males show up, staking their claims to mating and nesting territory. On a still Sunday afternoon, if you get far enough away from the road, the blackbirds are all you can hear, interrupted at intervals by somebody's church bell. It's a soothing environment, and Jack Curry wanted to be soothed. Instead, he drifted off slowly, along the stands of dried grasses and gone-wild thimbleberry bushes separating a pasture from a plowed field. And as he drifted, his plaque-clogged neurons began to transform southwestern Michigan into a strange amalgam of America and Southeast Asia.

A low hill separated him from the road, and it seemed that someone was trapped over there. On the other side of that hill, people he knew were in trouble. People were in danger. Someone had already been hurt. Jack began to breathe rapidly, and he tried to work the bolt on his rifle – but it wasn't an M-16, it was an old lever-action Winchester, and it didn't respond. His hand clawed at the side of the receiver, trying to work the action. His thumb touched the loading port, the dish-shaped gate through which rounds were loaded into the old gun's tube magazine, and somehow that brought back the right set of muscle memories. Instead of scrabbling for a bolt, his hand found the lever and racked it forward and back. A round slid back out of the magazine and cleanly up into the chamber. Jack broke into a run.

In the dining room, Jeanne Curry waved Clay to a seat at the table. At that moment, she still thought of him as their minister, still thought of him as someone on their side in an unequal contest with the world of finance and real estate. She was expecting to tell him that the current offer was acceptable and that she and Jack wanted to take it. She was ready, in fact, with an idea of paying Clay something for his work so far and letting him off the hook. It was a pity that he had to deal with all this, anyhow, especially today, since it was keeping him from the church, taking up his time with her problems, not letting him do the work he really wanted to do.

Now, though, Clay was acting differently than she'd seen before. He seemed excited, his voice was louder. He'd never spoken ill of people, any people, in her hearing. In church, the only thing he criticized was Satan; now, he was talking about the developers as 'bad people', people who wanted only one thing and that was to see honest, hard-working folks get taken to the cleaners. People who were out to make a quick dollar and nothing more. Well, Clay had an answer for them: over my dead body! He would see the Currys through this thing if he had to handle the development himself. Why, in fact, they could do it together! They could form a company, use the land to get loans, line up a good source of financing. What was standing in the way? Were we going to let those guys walk all over us?

Perhaps if Jeanne had had a few more exposures to inexpert sales pitches or used car dealers or hedge fund managers, she might not have been taken so much off guard. If Clay hadn't spent all those Sundays acting like a stolid, middle-class protestant preacher and pillar of the community, the new, evangelical Clay wouldn't have been such a surprise. But as it was, Jeanne had the sudden and frightening thought that he'd slipped a gear. Or worse, he'd been drinking. Her world and that of the people in the Lexus had no tangency at all. She couldn't even understand what Clay was suggesting, let alone imagine herself and John doing anything like it. Her goal was to get a big check and move south.

"But ... Reverend DeVoos, how long would that ... how much time ... we don't have any money saved up, really."

"Oh, yes you do, Jeanne," said Clay, the vision still with him. "Yes, you do. This land is your money, and with the land and my knowledge, we could make a partnership that would ... that would make you rich! You and John could do anything! Go anywhere! Be anything!" Of course, it was Clay he meant. With their land and his guiding hand on it, Clay was seeing himself doing things and being things. He had just enough self-control to say "you" instead of "we", but it was "we" and as matter of fact, "I", that he had in mind.

"Us? Building houses for people? We don't know anything about that! How would we ..." Jeanne was now standing, backing carefully away from the table, making sure she could get to the kitchen door if she had to.

"Oh, don't worry about all that," Clay said, his words running together in his eagerness to make a convert. "Eugene knows all that end of things. You know, he's got a construction company already. He's got the know-how, he can deal with it, no problem."

Of course, Jeanne knew Eugene, knew he was scarcely twenty, knew that his construction company was a parking space in the church's pole barn and a pickup truck with some hand tools in the back. He'd done a little work for the Currys once and did every minute of it himself. No employees, no subcontractors, and two or three trips to the hardware store, just to shore up a sagging porch. For Jeanne, Clay's rant had just gone way, way over the line in terms of credibility. And it was still going on, he was still talking about shares and getting financing and setting up an office in town. And he was on his feet now, too, and starting to take a step toward her. Her dismay turned instantly to fear, and her expression showed the fear.

And that, most unfortunately, was when Jack Curry came in the front door. There was a look of terror on his face, his mouth twisted with a kind of inward anguish. His boots were muddy from splashing across the little creek that ran through the east side of the farm, and his hands were scratched from the thimbleberry briars. In his mind, there was a terrible danger threatening people he loved.

"Jeanne!" he said, in a strangled voice. "Jeanne, Jeanne ... " And as Clay turned toward him, Jack fired one shot, straight into the side of Clay's head.

After all

> *"Listen to me, children, and we might yet get even*
> *With your criminal father for what he has done to us.*
> *After all, he started this whole ugly business."*

After the funeral, Eugene had to handle things by himself. Within a day of Clay's death, Eugene's mother moved back to *her* mother's house, and the very sight of Eugene would throw her into hysterics. They got her to sign a power of attorney, finally, for one of the brothers, on the promise that nobody from the DeVoos family would come anywhere near her again, and with that, the clan was able to settle up Clay's estate. His will was very simple, it turned out; everything went to the wife and son, equally, although there wasn't much to split up. He was not a very liquid man, and had never invested a dime in any kind of funds or stocks except, to everyone's surprise, in the family furniture store. Nobody would quite say how, but twenty-eight percent of the place actually belonged to Clay. The oldest of the brothers knew it, of course, since he dealt with the finances, but the other two were baffled and distinctly unhappy. Both of them suspected, quietly, that it was part of the original deal to get Clay off their payroll without scandal, but my Lord, more than a quarter of the value? Privately, they both thought the old boy had been a bit more wrapped up with Clay than he admitted, maybe a lot more wrapped up. While they thought about that and pondered ways of easing old brother Tom off into retirement so they could find out what the hell else he'd been up to, they did a certain amount of talking to Eugene about what he knew how to do and what he might like to do and how far away from Grand Rapids he'd be willing to do it. In the long run, as things just happened to work out, that was very unfortunate for Eugene.

As the business of the church was being shut down, so too Eugene was closing up his contracting business. This was primarily because he had no real customers except those his father's real estate work had pushed his way, and also because he suddenly felt a real and visceral desire to get out of town. He had enough of Clay's genome to know a bad situation when he saw it and enough of his mother's to be vaguely disturbed about what he and Clay had done. He didn't exactly feel guilty for trying to screw over the landowners, you understand, he was just shocked that anyone would think it was bad enough to shoot someone over. He did not buy the notion that Jack Curry was sick or crazy. He didn't believe what Mrs. Curry said about Clay wanting to start a development company. He did believe that something his father had done had gone badly wrong, and that Jack had shot him for it.

Eugene began to wake up in the night, remembering some silly thing he'd done himself and wondering who out there might be mad enough at him to do something about it. He thought about the Jack Currys in his brief set of acquaintances, and they made him nervous. So he shut down Eugene DeVoos Services, Inc., started telling people to call him 'Gene', and executed a Doing-Business-As under the name G. Hammersley Construction, Hammersley being Mom's maiden name. What the Hammersleys thought of this is not recorded.

As Gene was casting around for a way to make a living, Clay's second brother, Peter DeVoos, was having lunch at a diner up in Rockford. The gentleman seated next to him didn't look like one of the furies or a demon from hell. There was no reek of sulfur, no horns, no wings. In fact, he looked sort of respectable. He was late middle-aged, wearing slacks and a bomber jacket, a ball cap. After a few pleasantries, he said he was ex-military, retired from the defense business, and taking a while just to look around. But the plan was to settle down back at the family property in Sturgis, Michigan, down in Saint Joseph County: a hundred and twenty acres of farm land with a run-down house and a barn, plus a place next to a reasonably well travelled road that might pay the taxes if he could economize on the contracting enough to afford some kind of franchise: gas station, convenience store, something like that.

Gene's Uncle Peter was, as West Michigan small businessmen go, a pretty nice guy, mostly without malice, and he'd never done a violent thing in his life. But he took out a business card, wrote Gene's phone number on it, and handed it over. And with that act, Uncle Peter killed Gene DeVoos just as certainly as though he'd put a gun to his head and pulled the trigger himself.

Deep Currents

... Ocean with its deep currents ...

Sixty miles northeast of Ann Arbor, a blast of morning wind threw rain and sleet against the walls of the Macomb Correctional Facility. From above, the place looked like a cheaply-designed community college with Y-shaped blocks and criss-crossing sidewalks. From 26 Mile Road, it looked like nothing at all; trees, distance, and a kink in the driveway effectively concealed it.

Inside, unaffected by the weather, William McDivitt glared at his noisy cell mate and rolled over on his bunk to face the wall. Known on the street as Big Willy, he was the coke courier who had blown the Rome payoff case. Now, with his brother coming for a visit tomorrow, he needed to think about how the conversation would go. Big Willy was a smart guy for his age and circumstances, but he was in a tight corner. His brother, known (but not to his face) as Little Willy, was even smarter. Together, they'd figure something out.

From the Abyss

From the abyss were born Erebos and dark Night.

It was getting toward noon when MacArthur and Langton finished noting the facts, as known to that moment, about Rodney Garfield. Among the early data, of course, was the address of his parents, and that seemed like a good place to start looking for more. Mac sent Colleen a quick text message: *Won't be home at lunch time. Look at the Detroit news sites. Will IM if I can't make dinner.* An antenna van from the local

Fox station had been on site for a while, and Mac assumed that whatever was going to be released this early would be online by now. It was a round-about way of communicating, but Colleen was used to it, and it kept Mac from having to provide details when perhaps they shouldn't yet be provided.

The Feds stayed behind to confer with Chief Fredricks. Leg work such as notifying and interviewing the next of kin was a job they'd happily leave to locals. And so Mac and Langton took Jenn's department car and headed east to see Mr. and Mrs. Garfield. Rome was a twenty minute drive east on I-94, and if Jenn drove and did the introductions, they could probably avoid the question of Mac's status. In general, if two people show up to ask questions and one of them shows you a badge, it probably won't occur to you to care if the second person has one, too. But they did stop by Mac's house so that he could change into something slightly more cop-like.

"So we have a mother and a father in the house, hypothetically nobody else," Mac said, thinking out loud, visualizing how the encounter would go. It was a technique he'd tried to teach Jenn before, but he was never sure she understood it. She'd be focusing, he imagined, on the mother's reaction, the tears, the denial, the blame for the police for not preventing her son's death. She'd be wondering if someone would be drunk, maybe violent. Wondering if there'd be anyone else at the house.

Instead, Mac had tried to teach her to think of how *she'd* behave, how she, Langton, would react to hostility, to hysteria, to acceptance, and how she'd get the information they came to get, regardless of how the family took the news. It was sort of method acting for detectives. He'd run over the things they needed to know: when Rodney left the house, if he left with someone, if there'd been recent trouble, who he hung out with and where, if there was a girlfriend. That was always a good one, and it frequently led somewhere. Here, though, he doubted that it would. Girl trouble might lead to a quick, heat of the moment shooting. (There had actually been an out-and-out feud in one of the townships the previous summer, over girls and boys and their relationships). But although sex could easily lead to drive-bys and knifings and fist fights, it was unlikely to lead to a boy restrained, shot twice in the head, and dumped in a strange city, in a strange place. No, this talk with Rodney's parents, taken down to its simplest, was going to be a matter of saying, "Your son's been murdered. We're sorry. What can you tell us to make our job easier?"

Langton was in fact thinking, as Mac assumed, about the unpleasantness. She was deeply uncomfortable with notifying next of kin, probably, she admitted, as a result of her years' worth of experience expecting to be notified herself. She'd done this kind of visit a dozen times or more, though never as a result of a homicide. She'd brought news of death from many other causes: auto accidents, overdoses, heart attacks, the grind of life among the unlucky. People screamed, wept, went silent, looked for someone to blame. If they were high or drunk, there was a physical hazard, and there was always the question whether they'd heard you, whether they'd wake up the next day and remember what they'd been told. So although she was listening to Mac, what he was saying wasn't working out as a lesson in an aspect of police work, it was filtering through her own ways of thinking, amplifying and feeding on the anxiety.

The house was the last one on the street before residential buildings gave way to commercial. It was a single story box, seven hundred square feet if that, with a one-bay garage attached to the south side. The driveway was asphalt, cracked and being encroached upon by the grass and groundcover at its edges. Beyond the house to the south, there was a vacant lot and then the back of a convenience store. Mac heaved himself out of the passenger's door and looked carefully around: no cars in the driveway, none on the street, and opposite the house, just a patch of trees and weeds that looked as though they extended through to the next block. The nearest house was close on the north side, larger, better kept, and with a silver minivan in the drive. No one was outside, and the only traffic was on the cross street, seventy-five yards away.

They knocked, and after a minute or two, a black woman in her late forties answered. Too soon and too fast, Jenn had her badge out, thinking of it as a shield in more than a symbolic way. For her, it said "I'm a cop, respect me, listen carefully to me, don't attack me. I'm allowed to be here and to ask you questions." But for Mrs. Amanda Garfield, it just said, "Trouble. Again."

"Can I help you?" she asked.

"Are you Mrs. Garfield?" Jenn asked. "Did you turn in a missing person report on Rodney Garfield?"

"Yeah, I did. Or my husband did. He call the police. You find the boy?"

"Mrs. Garfield, I'm sorry for your loss, ma'am. I'm afraid Rodney Garfield may be dead," Jenn said, bringing it out in one flat sequence and getting it slightly wrong; you're supposed to say "Sorry for your loss," after you say the victim is dead, not before. But it wouldn't have mattered.

Amanda's face cleared of all expression, going blank. Her eyes went straight past Jenn, past Mac, out into the overgrown lot next door, someplace with no humanity in it, no people to see and no one to look back.

"Well, it don't surprise me none," she said.

It took an hour and a half to finish the process of explaining that the body of a young man, very close to the description of her son that Mr. Garfield had given the Wayne County Sheriff's office, had been found; that someone, preferably Mr. or Mrs. Garfield, would need to come into Ann Arbor and identify the body; and to ask the necessary questions about who and why and when. They searched Rodney's room, too. There was nothing useful, no wallet, no iPhone, no guns or drugs. No suicide note. Either his life had been remarkably free of material possessions, or he'd taken them with him.

As Mac and Jenn drove back toward the highway, Mac was marking up his handwritten notes, adding things he'd failed to write down, and talking at the same time. It was something he always did, even if he was alone after an interview. It helped fix the information in his mind.

"So, Rodney was at home last night until ten o'clock, at least. That's when Mom and Dad went to bed, she says. This morning, he wasn't around, nothing gone except the clothes he was wearing. Neither of them heard anything. Mom thinks he may have gone out the window of his room, since the outside doors were locked, and she says he didn't have any keys."

"And they called him in right away because he was on parole," Jenn said, "Not supposed to be out of the house at night. Not because they were afraid something had happened."

"Right. They wanted him violated and sent back to jail. Get him out of the place, stop having to listen to him whine and carry on."

"No current girlfriends," said Jenn. "I got the impression that was one of the things he was whining about."

"Yup," said Mac. "No girlfriends and not a lot of friends of any kind ... not since he got out of Wayne County, anyway. Somebody there didn't care for him, either." One of the things his mother had mentioned was that Rodney had taken a beating in jail, officially at the hands of another inmate. Mac had nothing in particular to say about that. Either it was true or it wasn't; if the kid had anything like the attitude his mother described, it wouldn't be hard to imagine anyone, an inmate or a correctional officer or even a deputy giving him a lesson in behavior. But it would be highly necessary to follow it up; from a beating to a shooting was a short step.

"We don't like the parents for this, right?" Jenn asked.

"The parents? Well, I don't see it," said Mac. "We still have to talk to the father, but I doubt it." *We need to run down their backgrounds, too*, he thought. *And what do I mean, 'we', Kemosabe? She's the one who has to make up her mind about that. I'm retired, damn it, and the AAPD can at least do its own record checks.*

Still, it'd take a big, big smoking gun to get Mac to think of this case as a simple family thing. They'd have thrown the kid out in the street, maybe, thrown his clothes after him, told him to get lost. They might even have killed him, especially if somebody had been drinking, but it wouldn't have been an execution — not unless somebody involved was a lot smarter and more inherently evil-seeming than the mother. As for the father, William Garfield: well, they'd have to see, but the whole atmosphere of the house said "poverty" very loudly. And people scraping by on three and a half jobs between two aging adults don't have the time or the expertise to plan a professional hit. They kill, sometimes, when they're angry or intoxicated or both, but they do it wildly, randomly, and without much of a plan. *And if I think anything at all about this yet*, Mac thought, *I think there was a plan.*

Epimetheus

> *... witless Epimetheus,*
> *Who was trouble from the start ...*

The tipping point for Robert Dwayne Hagland was usually four beers. He was a cheap date, in the sunk cost sense of the word, although he frequently cost quite a lot in liability, long term debt, and loss of good will. Extensive and repeated exposure to alcohol, by the way, does *not* increase tolerance, or if it does,

Hagland represented an outlier in the statistics. After experimenting for a while with methamphetamine, he'd come to the conclusion that in terms of return on investment, beer was a better strategy. He was not one of the demographic to which American light beers are advertised, nor the people that Sam Adams and Dos Equis are aiming for; he was a drinker-without-portfolio, not at all brand-conscious, and perfectly ready to drink whatever was available for an acceptably low price per unit.

He was a large individual, with a long-cycle skinhead presentation, meaning that most of the time, his shaven skull was two or three days overdue for a shave and exhibited a sixteenth-inch of blond stubble all over. He was an ill-educated, low-IQ, child-left-behind, showing the effects of both poor nature *and* nurture, and one of the people least likely ever to vote, file an income tax return, or live past thirty-five. His job skills were nil, his resume a blank page, and his criminal record a collection of the kind of nuisance crimes that take up most of a local police department's time. He did have a kind of intuitive ability to keep a car running by applying band aids of one kind or another, without actually fixing any underlying problems. Early in his teens, he'd forfeited the rights to possess firearms and to drive, and of course now, at age twenty-eight, he possessed a number of guns and regularly drove around the southwest suburbs and outlying counties, drinking, carrying on, causing trouble of a minor sort, and generally being a jackass. Periodically, a new acquaintance — someone who hadn't known him for long — would hire him off the books to do something menial. Between that and selling a bit of weed, he had beer and gas money; bed and board came from his parents, whose basement he occupied.

The problem with Hagland was that he wasn't quite enough of an idiot. He was dimly aware that his personal situation wasn't as good as it could be. Speaking of him having ambition, per se, would have been inaccurate, but he did have a kind of veiled desire to have more money week to week and a more expensive truck. Women he had already, to the extent that he could stay sober enough to meet them, discriminate among them based on the size and fearsomeness of their male companions, and convince them to go for rides and/or buy a baggie or two. But in his more lucid moments, he did recognize that a larger income would improve his general satisfaction with life.

For a while, that just led him to experiment with larger-scale dealing in marijuana, but the stumbling block there was the need for investment capital. That in turn led to a few ventures into grand-theft-auto, but the chop shops weren't sanguine about doing business with a punk from Milan who didn't know enough to pry the VIN tags off the cars before he tried to sell them. Two or three of the more paranoid gangs decided that he was undercover and refused to talk to him, let alone buy anything. And since these individuals happened to be black, it just reinforced Hagland's bred-in racism: "A white guy can't get a break now," was the most coherent expression of his feelings on the topic. Gradually he began to do his drinking farther and farther west, out into the still-rural, extremely white parts of southern Michigan, where the remaining farms were big, but the average guy lived in a small house next to a two-lane road, and if he had a job, he drove fifty or sixty miles one way to get to it. The towns were depressed and depressing, and the bars were unsophisticated, slab-sided, and ugly, like a lot of the people. It was a comfortable environment for a guy like Bobby, and he began to be a regular at a number of saloons, taps, and biker bars from Tecumseh to Coldwater, Sherwood, Colon, and Sturgis (City motto: Not *That* Sturgis.) Nevertheless, there wasn't a lot of money to be made out there, for someone with his skills, and he found that he still had to go back into the Detroit suburbs periodically, just to top up his meager inventory of weed.

That was what he'd had in mind, one evening in October, when he'd taken the keys to his brother's truck and driven away from the parental farmhouse, headed for Rome. His brother Frank was serving in Afghanistan; Bobby liked to use Frank's truck for his wholesale purchasing expeditions on the absurd theory that if he had to run from the police, they'd waste time looking for Frank first, giving him, Bobby, time to hide his various illegal possessions before they got around to him. This was fallacious reasoning, since Frank had no record and could be almost instantly shown to be on the other side of the planet, whereas Bobby was known to any number of local police agencies and would be the obvious person to seek out. But optimism and a kind of mystical reliance on luck was a part of his makeup, and anyway, his own pickup was low on gas.

He drove north on US 23, then east on 94 toward the airport and an appointment with a colleague in the business. That person lived on the north side of the highway, opposite Metro, and so Bobby got off on Haggerty Road, then went north to Tyler, east again from there over 275, and so down into an as-yet-underdeveloped strip of road. A mile or so past the freeway overpass, there was a small church with a cemetery, and that was where he'd arranged to meet his supplier. It was a quick exchange, dollars for merchandise, conducted from one driver's-side window to another. Each party knew the other, and there was no discussion of terms and conditions. The seller, his vehicle now empty of anything illegal, would wait a few minutes; Hagland left at once, leaving his lights off until he was out the drive and back on the road. So far, it had been a surgically precise operation.

But Bobby's life was not one of ongoing surgical precision, especially when he was making things up as he went along. It now occurred to him that perhaps a beer might be a good thing, and if it could be arranged, a chat with a woman he knew in Rome, now just a bit to the southeast. And so as he drove, he placed a call, left a message on an answering machine, and instead of heading back to Milan and his father's old tool shed (where he hid his stash), he drove east to Hannan Road, turned south and back under 94, and then went east on a road called Southline. After a bit, Southline intersects at a sharp angle with Huron River Drive, and not too far down Huron River Drive is a small establishment called The Shed. Alcohol and light refreshment were available there, and it was in The Shed that Bobby had suggested meeting his friend.

Although there's no good way to tell except by looking at a property tax bill, The Shed was just within the city limits of Rome, and for that reason the Rome police, those that were not under indictment, kept an eye on it. Beside the fact that its patrons were occasionally disorderly and sometimes highly intoxicated when they drove away (and everybody drove; Rome was not a walkable city, really), its parking lot was also a good turn-around spot for the cops as they came to the end of their jurisdiction. As a result, the chance of a Rome police car driving in and out of The Shed's Huron River Drive frontage was greater than just about any other drinking place in town. This was not something Bobby knew.

However, to partly justify his faith in luck, there was no place left to park in the bar's small lot. Nor was there a spot at the convenience store across the street. So Bobby drove past and pulled into the empty lot of a plumbing supply store, ninety yards farther on. He secured his marijuana under the seat of the truck, locked everything up, and hiked back to The Shed. Just as he walked up to the door, Officer Richard Jastrimski cruised by in his Crown Victoria.

Jastrimski was one of the guys who'd been kept out of the drug payoff deal. He was new; he talked a lot, like an interviewee on a reality show, about being in law enforcement to help people; and he was generally distrusted by the older, dirtier members of the Rome force. When the roof fell in, Dick J. as they called him had been appalled, angry, ashamed, and ready to quit. But he hadn't found a new job yet, he had a new baby to support, and he felt a need to keep on being an effective cop. He was a man with something to prove.

A month ago, he'd pulled Bobby Hagland over for an illegal right turn on red, and Hagland had shown some attitude. He got the ticket and, worse, he got his face recorded in Dick J.'s young and capable memory. Now Dick J. had just seen that same wise-ass son-of-a-bitch go into The Shed.

Dick thought fast as he rolled on by. He couldn't just go in and kick ass. The man hadn't done anything patently illegal so far. And he was just going in; maybe he hadn't had a chance to get drunk yet. So Dick would give him a chance to have a couple of drinks and then come out and drive away. When he did, Dick would be waiting, pull him over, and see if the boy could recite the ABCs backward. Worst case, he'd get to jack Hagland around; best case, he'd really be drunk, maybe have a weapon or some dope. Make a nice little arrest out of what was so far a slow evening. And so Dick glanced at his watch and noted that it was eight-fifteen. At eight-thirty or eight-forty-five, he'd come back by again and see what was happening.

Bobby, for his part, was not looking for cop cars. He was looking for the new Chevy that another man's wife drove around to various bars while her husband was working a night shift. However, there was no such car in the lot. Not too surprised — she hadn't returned his call — Bobby went into The Shed. Inside, there were ten or fifteen tables, a dance floor, and a bar. He slid onto a stool at the bar, nodded to the patron next to him, and ordered a beer.

The fellow next to Bobby was wearing a ball cap with a GOP elephant logo and the message, 'Buck Ofama', and Bobby had to think about that for a minute or so before he got it. Although he had no personal politics whatsoever, his general attitude toward the world positioned him as a supporter of anything opposed to liberals, Democrats, and black presidents. "Pretty funny," he said, gesturing toward the hat. The other customer had been in the bar since four-thirty and had nothing coherent to say at all on any topic. He had, in fact, forgotten that he was wearing a hat. The guy's jacket identified him as a member of a union, but the irony of his two sartorial messages struck neither party. The conversation went nowhere.

Some sporting event was playing on the bar's television set. It might have been hockey, but since it didn't involve stock cars or trucks or explosions, Bobby wasn't all that interested. Time passed; he watched the TV idly, while also eyeing the door to see if Amber was going to show up. Instead, when the door did finally open, an older man came in. He said to the bartender, "That damn cop is parked outside again."

This piece of intelligence provoked two very different responses within the bar. The bartender, who was in his late forties, big, with a shaved head and a handlebar mustache, reacted with pique: "That little asshole!" It was his thesis that the police, especially the youthful and enthusiastic Officer Dick J., were constantly harassing his customers, denying them their constitutionally-guaranteed right to drive while two or three times over the legal limit. Worse than that, not only were the customers inconvenienced (and the barkeep had to admit that some of them were assholes, too), but the cops then came back and harassed *him* for continuing to serve people who were too drunk to walk, let alone drive. He and the bar's owner had complained effectively to police management in the past, but then the police management had all been arrested themselves, and recent complaints were falling on deaf ears. So the news that there was a Rome police car in his parking lot was not soothing.

For Bobby Hagland, though, the report sparked not anger but concern, bordering on fear. He remembered with a start just what was under the front seat of his brother's pickup truck, for one thing, and for another his recent encounter with the local cops in this fair city. That they were specifically looking for him seemed unlikely, but their presence was also not a desirable thing. In fact, any proximity to a uniformed person was something to be avoided by a man with weed, no driver's license, and a small handgun in a jacket pocket. He hadn't had enough to drink so far this evening that his native tactical cunning was too far gone, and instead of panicking, he actually stopped to think.

Bobby was not commonly a methodical thinker. Science-based anything wasn't part of his usual approach to determining a course of action or forming an opinion, and his mental image of a scientist was a cartoon figure with glasses and a lab coat — or Thomas Dolby. The structured and objective evaluation of hypotheses, using carefully observed data, if he'd ever heard anyone suggest it, would have struck him as fighting words. In fact, if you'd assured him that his life depended on answering the question, "What is scientific method?" he might have been able to come up with, "You know, chemicals and shit."

In a situation like this, though, there were few enough variables that he could juggle the facts around and come up with at least a short term plan. For one thing, he hadn't parked in the lot; if he decided to bet on the cop's simply being out there looking for drunks, he could just sit in here until the cruiser drove away. But if they *were* looking for him, they'd come in and he'd be a sitting duck. So perhaps the best thing to do would be to fade away, somehow, without going out that front door.

Bobby dug out a few dollars, set them on the bar, and headed back to the men's room. It was, as usual in establishments like The Shed, at the back, and to his gratification there was also a back door. It had a knob lock, plus a hasp and padlock, but up until closing, fire regulations prevented it from being secured. He slipped out and looked around. It was dark enough, but the bar was a standalone building, with fifteen feet or so of open space separating it from the owner's small house in the next lot. That gap in cover was between Bobby and the direction he had to go to skirt behind the buildings and get back to his truck. He crossed it in a kind of nervous, I'm-not-hurrying shuffle, which drew the attention of Dick J., sitting out in his cruiser, just as he'd decided to forget about the whole thing and drive away. He only glimpsed Bobby for a second, but he saw the movement and registered it as suspicious. Instead of getting out, though, he started the car and backed up, planning on driving back behind the bar.

That alerted Bobby Hagland, and in the seconds that the officer was focused on not backing out into the street, he vanished behind the small house. He cut sharply to his right and ran back up a driveway toward the street. Part way there, he broke left into the trees in front of the next house, sprinted around it to the left, and pulled up, breathing hard, behind another tree, looking out on the lot where the pickup was sitting. He heard gravel crunching as the cop car stopped, two hundred feet back. He heard the door slam and the officer shouting, presumably at him. Obviously, though, he couldn't be seen, and the moment seemed right. He sprinted to the truck, fumbled the door unlocked and open, and jumped in.

He had just enough sense not to pull straight out onto Huron River Drive. Instead, he drove back behind the plumbing store, then out the exit of a car wash and north on a side street, taking a quick right at the first opportunity. This brought him out onto the main drag in Rome, Von Braun Street, which was not the best place to be, assuming somebody was looking for him in a vehicle. If not, if the cop was still back there looking for a pedestrian, then he was more or less home free, as long as he could get the hell out of Dodge without running across any more police. But driving down the main street probably wasn't the right thing to do.

He froze, mentally, torn between the desire for dark side streets and the idea that absolute stealth lay in doing nothing unusual. In that mode, he drove on down Von Braun until it suddenly turned on him, bending beyond ninety degrees to the right to avoid a railroad crossing. He went with it and was now headed due east, not at all a useful direction for him, given that he really wanted to be going southwest out of town. Still paranoid, he passed up a couple of turns out of sheer inability to decide, then impulsively turned left up a side street, headed back toward the railroad. The street lasted a block before it came to a grade crossing. The railroad here was double tracked, and somehow the distance between the two beds of ties and ballast suggested a course of action. With little or no thought at all, Bobby turned hard left, putting one set of wheels between each pair of rails, and drove west right down the tracks.

Meanwhile, out behind The Shed, Officer Jastrimski was having a conversation with the bartender who had come outside to express his concern over community policing methods. The general tenor of the discussion revolved around property rights, whether or not there had been any goddamn complaint filed about prowlers or other people behind the building, the names and telephone numbers of police supervisors, and the formality or lack thereof of Jastrimski's parents' marital relationship. Dick J. got back in his car, closely followed by the tapster who had not yet exhausted his talking points. Dick backed up out of the situation; he was pretty sure that either the guy he was after or somebody else doing something sketchy was on foot back here, and he also knew that the options for parking a vehicle were limited, in the direction his subject had been heading. So he drove east, more or less as Bobby had, and turned down Von Braun. He was about three minutes behind Bobby, in fact, but out of sight on the main street, when Bobby took his detour down the railroad.

The lack of lights or sirens behind him did a certain amount to restore Bobby's normal margin of self-control, which is to say, he became suddenly aware that driving down railroad tracks in a truck with a half-kilo of weed was patently insane. He was going quite slowly and had only moved about a block west. A cross street appeared, one that had been truncated by the railroad but never very well blocked off, and Bobby wrenched the truck off the tracks, bouncing wildly, and got back onto pavement, Silver Street, headed back toward Von Braun and back south in a direction that would eventually lead him out of Rome. As he approached the intersection with Von Braun, Jastrimski drove across it.

In fact, he didn't initially notice Bobby's truck, because he didn't know what he was looking for. But Bobby saw him, panicked for real this time, failed to stop, and rolled right on through, still headed south. *That* Dick J. did see, in his mirror, and he braked hard, intending to make a U-turn and go back for a traffic stop. A parked car interfered with his maneuver, though, and by the time Dick had gotten turned around, Bobby had cut a corner through a medical clinic parking lot, gone west a block and then headed south. Jastrimski could see no pickup at this point, but he hit his lights and siren, guessed wrong and turned east, and never saw the truck again. Bobby got out of town to the south, eventually making a long drive of it on back roads, and he parked the truck out of sight behind his father's barn. Dick Jastrimski, having had an annoyingly bad night of it, went back and looked up Hagland's name and other vital statistics from the previous traffic stop. He filed on Hagland for fleeing and eluding. That he had no real proof that Bobby was driving that pickup truck seemed unimportant. For the moment, quiet settled over the land. It was illusory, though. There would be repercussions.

King Pelias

... the outrageously arrogant,
Presumptuous bully, King Pelias ...

From his parents' house near Milan, the western limit of Bobby's wanderings was ninety miles in a straight line. The terminus of that line was the town of Sturgis, Michigan, but for plenty of tactical, economic, and geographic reasons, there was no good way to drive there on a single compass bearing. Instead, the real distance was half again as much, if, as Bobby did, you followed mostly state and county two-lane roads. Doing that, you would pass through increasingly rural territory in five counties: Monroe, Lenawee, Branch, Hillsdale, and Saint Joseph.

All of them were border counties, separating the rest of Michigan from Ohio and Indiana. Another pair of things they had in common was that, as you got further west, they had smaller populations and far less rural policing. By the time you got to Saint Joseph County, for example, you were in a county with only sixty-two thousand people, all told. Each of the towns represented a large chunk of that number, and so, to the extent they could afford it, they provided a similar chunk of the county-wide law enforcement; the county sheriff's department was quite small and mostly concerned with the jail. As a result, your risk of a routine traffic stop was very low indeed, if you travelled the back roads, and that's how Bobby tended to go, to the greatest extent he could.

Forty-eight hours after his daring escape from Rome, Bobby arranged to transfer some of his inventory to a man he'd met in a bar in Colon, Michigan. Colon was twelve miles or so north of Sturgis, but the buyer was actually from Shipshewana, down across the line in Indiana. They agreed to meet in Sturgis, at a bar just off the main street. As he drove down, Bobby got a call from his associate, saying that the bar was closed due to a fire, and that they could just meet up outside an old theatre on US 12, The Beach. Bobby was generally familiar with it, and without giving much, or in fact any, thought to security, he agreed.

As always when engaged on business, Bobby was well-equipped. Beside the small amount of product in question, he had a thirty-two caliber pistol with which, on a good day, he could easily hit the broad side of a barn two out of three times; a poorly faked ID card identifying him as someone else; and a six pack of inexpensive beer. He was wearing his usual outfit: a sleeveless T-shirt, a long-sleeved flannel shirt over it, jeans, running shoes, and a nylon jacket. A Detroit Tigers ball cap, worn fashionably backward, completed the look. Having a good deal of time on his hands during the day, he'd taken the trouble to break down an ounce of marijuana into small, ten-dollar-sized parcels, and he had them loose in a jacket pocket. This was not a matter of good customer service but rather a method that would make it possible to short the buyer a bag or two, if he wasn't paying close attention.

Bobby drove down into Sturgis on M-66, through a mixed residential and commercial neighborhood, past sign shops, tire stores, mom and pops of various kinds. There was a railroad crossing with its uncomfortable reminder of the Rome adventure, the Sturgis police department, and then the big intersection with US 12: downtown Sturgis. He turned right, and within a block he could see the vertical sign for The Beach theater. And as he rolled up, there was the bright red Dodge Ram belonging to his customer, a fellow he knew as 'Jim'.

The trouble was, Jim had his Dodge parked in the last legal space on the street; the whole rest of the block was lined off as no parking, providing a drop off and pick up zone for the theater. Bobby didn't notice that or maybe didn't care, and he pulled in ahead of his friend's truck, shut off his own old Ford pickup, and got out. He walked up to the driver's door of the Ram and began the simple mechanics of a hand-to-hand drug deal. This was not the obvious tip-off it might have been elsewhere; in Sturgis, people did actually talk innocently to each other in public, and the police would not consider it unusual. But the Sturgis officer who was sitting on the next cross street, waiting for the light to change, did notice the illegal parking job. He turned right, putting himself across US-12 from The Beach, and pulled to the curb. Bobby's back was turned, leaning in the truck window, but Jim saw the cop and said, predictably, "Oh, shit! The cops!"

If this incident was ever to be subjected to any kind of careful analysis, which it was certainly not, those sifting through it might wonder whether Bobby's contact spoke out of simple reaction or whether it was intended to produce the outcome it did. Regardless, the results were good from Jim's standpoint, since it caused Bobby to instinctively pull back his hand, still holding all the weed packets, and take off running eastward up the street. This in turn led the officer to leap out of his car, shouting "Stop!" and to dash off after Bobby. Jim dropped the Dodge into drive, turned north at the first chance, then west, then south, and went as fast as he prudently could back out of town and back into Indiana, weedless but with his money in hand and criminal record unenhanced.

Meanwhile, Bobby exploited his half-block lead on the law by turning north up a side street, flinging his handgun as far and as hard as he could up onto the roof of a one-story florist shop, and cutting right behind an empty building. As he ran, he dropped one baggie after another, like an orphan dropping bread crumbs, and by the time the pursuing officer got a clear sight line on him, he was down to a single parcel. He gave up at that point, falling back on the tried and true, "I didn't do nothing wrong!" defense, and was cuffed, transported, and jailed. In the morning, once his actual identity had been established, he would have been able to bond out on a simple possession charge had not Rome officer Jastrimski's charge of fleeing and eluding turned up on the computer. Instead of scuffling around getting his truck out of hock and driving home, Bobby spend another night in the Saint Joe jail, and then he got a ride back to the metro area for a date with the authorities in Wayne County. Although he did eventually get out on bond, the whole thing added up to enough bad karma for Bobby that when he came to trial, he was sentenced to three months in Wayne County's Division III lockup, down in beautiful Hamtramck. Although any kind of wise jail administration policy would have taken one look at someone like Bobby Hagland and quickly found him a cell with other shaved-head white boys, mistakes do happen, and he found himself sharing quarters with a young black man named Rodney Garfield.

There are ideal pairings in the set of human personalities, two people who seem destined to complement each other, to multiply each other's strengths and overlook shortcomings, friendships, so to speak, that are pre-ordained. Bobby and Rodney were not such a pair. Each one carried a large, splintery chip on his shoulder, and the only important difference was that Bobby was physically equipped to do something about it, and Rodney was not. Another key point was that each was, in his separate way, a racist. Bobby had a grudge against the smarter, more professional criminals he'd come in contact with, most of whom had written him off as a bad risk, and for no particular reason, these people had been mostly black. On top of that specific complaint, he'd absorbed the classic poor white boy's mistaken idea that minorities were somehow favored by the system.

For his part, Rodney had been brought up in a home where his black parents worked for white people and were paid poorly and treated worse. Comfort and choices were missing, largely, from his life so far, and though he might not have said, "This would be different if I were white," it was apparent to him that not being black would very likely have improved things. Every source of information he had, from the media to his fellow high

73

school students, had contributed to that feeling. And it didn't help that the last three times he'd been arrested, the police officers had been white and unresponsive to his version of "I didn't do nothing."

And so, from the first time Bobby was introduced into their shared cell, each one began to exercise his attitude. Rodney, who had neither bulk nor technique on his side, had been forced to adopt a threatening, street-kid pose from age seven on, and it was his only resource, his only trick. Hagland, on the other hand, didn't need tricks; he could mop the floor with someone Rodney's size, and he did, as soon as the correctional officers were out of sight. 'Mop the floor' was not really a good description of the technique; 'wipe the wall' would be more accurate, since anything like a wise-sounding remark from Rodney would usually result in Bobby spinning the kid around by the shoulders, grabbing his neck in both hands, lifting him six or eight inches straight up off his feet, and shoving him against the wall. He would hold this position until choking noises indicated submission. A kick in the buttocks then set a period on the lesson.

Bobby managed to do this and keep on doing it for nearly twenty straight days, without being observed by authority and without leaving obvious marks, right up to the day they told him he was getting out early, due to overcrowding. In his last half hour in jail, just for old times' sake, he smacked Rodney around in a manner that left him bruised and huddled on his bunk. Hagland then said goodbye and was released to his long-suffering father. Not surprisingly, in all the time they spent together, neither Bobby nor Rodney had learned anything about the other, including any details at all of past lives and the various crimes that had brought them together.

Bobby sat quietly at home for the next few days, assessing the efficiency of his new parole officer, and when the data indicated that he was unlikely even to see this individual, let alone be ambushed by her, he began to plan another trip west. During his time in jail, he'd thought over the Sturgis event, and he'd come to the conclusion that Indiana Jim had set him up. There was no good reason for him to think so, but it felt better than blaming himself for committing an incompetent crime. He began to elaborate on the plot, and he came to the conclusion that Jim needed a whuppin', if it could be accomplished without serious risk to himself. He'd met Jim in a bar in Colon, so his entire plan consisted of revisiting that bar and seeing if the guy was there. If he was, Bobby'd act friendly, lure Jim outside, and give him some of what he'd been giving Rodney.

To get there and to get anywhere else, in fact, he would have to appropriate brother Frank's truck again. His had been seized by the Sturgis police. Although Bobby resented that on principle, it had been in terrible shape, and he was saved the trouble of fixing or scrapping it himself. Except for a bit of a flutter in the front end, probably due to the railroad detour, Frank's Chevrolet S-10 was newer and sounder and used less gas than the old Ford, anyway.

Of course, the terms of his parole did not allow him to do anything at all like driving halfway across the state, after hours, to visit a bar with intent to commit assault. Also obviously, his parents were aware of that, but their ability to keep him from doing it was nil. He was a big boy. He had never actually kicked his father's ass or his mother's for that matter, but it was obvious that he could. Both of them had noticed, too, that when Bobby was in jail, things at the old homestead were quieter, safer, and generally better. If Bobby were to do something stupid and illegal again and get caught, neither of the old folks would shed a tear.

So when he decided to go, he just got up and went. Keys to the truck were not a problem, since he had several sets concealed around the place. As he retrieved one of them from under a coffee can in the shed, he also picked up the three ten-dollar bills he'd left there, and then he emptied the can out onto an open space on a shelf. Under a layer of assorted nuts and bolts, there was another small handgun. He thought about it a bit, but then pocketed it. His .32 was probably still on the roof of a pharmacy, after all, and there wasn't any way he was going to get that back. This second gun was even less impressive – a four-barrel reproduction of an old .22 caliber gambler's weapon – but it was, in Bobby's view, better than nothing, and he'd gone to a certain amount of trouble to swindle one of his customers out of it. Geared up, he drove the truck out from behind the barn and headed off. He had a few bucks, and he was not carrying any of his remaining stash, since he was just bright enough to keep sales trips and ass-kicking trips separate. He'd stop for beef jerky and a six pack, and what more could a man need?

The Barren, Raging Sea

Then she gave birth to the barren, raging Sea ...

Mac and Jenn dialed into the conference call from a meeting room in the new city hall. On the other end, Doug and Andy Patel were in Doug's office, downtown in Detroit. The Feds' con-call system was at least theoretically secure, and although the whole discussion only cost about twelve dollars less than it would have driving to a meeting, everybody felt greener about it.

Who's-on-that-end? questions having been dealt with, Doug asked what they found out in Rome.

"Well," said Langton, "We went out there and a couple of other places, too, and here's what we came up with. Mom and Dad don't really have alibis, but Mac and I think they're a really long shot. Very unlikely to have done anything like this, and especially not this way."

"Yeah, Doug," said Mac. "This is not a killer pair. They were fed up with the victim, but I got nothing that sniffed like violence. They'd have turned him in for parole violations in a heartbeat, but I don't see them shooting him."

"Okay, go ahead."

"The main impression we got from them," said Jenn, "was the lack ... I guess you'd say the complete lack ... of *any* impression. They didn't know who his friends were. They just knew that when he hung around with people, they got him in trouble. They didn't know about any girlfriend, about any girls at all, really ..."

"Um, wait a minute," said Doug. "What kind of trouble did his buddies get him into?"

"Minor stuff. He's been popped three times for personal-use quantities of weed. The last time, he ran, and that got him done for fleeing."

"But drugs, though? He knew people who were into drugs?"

"Well, yeah," said Mac, "If you call one baggie at a time of cheap marijuana, 'drugs'."

"Okay. Got it. What else?"

"Well," said Jenn, "We wanted to hear more about all that, obviously, so we tried calling the school he went to ... before he dropped out." That had been Mac's idea. "We talked to the one teacher who remembered him, and that guy remembered one other kid's name that Rodney hung out with. We tracked him down, and guess what? He's in jail, right here at Washtenaw County, for a domestic."

"Really?" said Doug. "That's convenient."

"Yeah, it was. So we dropped in on him on our way back. He was talky, kind of freaked out about the killing. Happy to talk to us, it seemed like."

What they'd heard from the young man was essentially the same profile of Rodney that his parents provided, except with more detail. He was not a bright person, not a lot of fun to be with, big attitude but nothing to back it up. Not an ambitious criminal, either, and he never had any money, never had a ride, always bumming a cigarette or some weed, a beer or two. If he'd ever had a job, nobody knew about it. The inevitable question about who'd want to kill him drew a complete blank. But then, Mac had asked about the beating in jail.

Yes, their informant had heard about that, from Rodney, in detail. No, he didn't know anything about the guy who did it, some white guy. But he did mention another person who knew Rodney and who'd gotten shoved around by a white guy on the street, a while back. Could it be the same one? He didn't know, but he gave them the victim's name.

"We're tracking that one down, still," said Jenn.

"You think it might be the same guy?" asked Andy. "The same one, Hagland, is it? who was in jail with our victim? Sorry, *your* victim."

"I think we really need to talk to this Robert Hagland," said Doug. "I'd like to know how he got into the cell assignment with Garfield."

"Yup," said Mac. "And you know, I think you guys might have a bit more luck with that than we would. You know people at Wayne Three, right? I don't know anybody down there at all."

"Yeah," said Doug. "We can work that end of it. Can you try to find Hagland himself?"

"Yes, we'll work on that," said Jenn. "We have an address. He's on paper for his last conviction, so he's supposed to be living with his parents, down in Milan. I have a call in to his parole officer, but nothing back so far."

"You know, a couple of things about this occur to me," said Mac. "Maybe a little over-thought, but see how this strikes you. If there's any, oh, let's say, 'serious' aspects to the shooting, well, I seem to remember some things going on in Rome where a lot of people on one side of a deal got busted ..." He paused to see if he was going too far.

"Yeah," said Doug. Non-committal.

"Well, I don't remember that much of anyone on the other side was indicted." Langton was staring at him, confused. He scribbled 'later' on a pad and showed it to her.

"So, I'm thinking maybe some of those other people are interested in keeping it that way."

"I've had that thought, too," said Doug.

"And that led me to a sort of fork in the road. Two ways it could go. Maybe our victim was killed to keep something secret. If a nobody like that knew it, probably other people know it, too. So if we stir things up too much, we might have some other people shot."

"Okay," said Doug. "Maybe."

"Or, and this is the other path, maybe Rodney was shot to send a message about keeping your mouths shut. And that way, the more noise we make, the more people get the message and the less we hear."

"So, regardless, we keep a low profile," said Andy.

"Yeah," said Doug. "We do."

"So my thought," said Mac, "Is that if we can find Hagland, we just chat about whether his poor murdered cell mate told him anything while they were together. If he's ... serious ... enough to get himself busted and then jailed with a specific person, he'll be capable of vanishing too if he gets a hint that we like him for the shooting."

79

They finished the call with agreement that Doug and Andy would see what the Wayne County corrections people could tell them about Hagland, and that Mac and Jenn would go see Bobby himself, if he was living where he was supposed to be. Jenn hung up the phone.

"What was all that business about 'serious'?" she asked.

"Sorry. I forgot you weren't in the airport discussion with Doug." Mac gave Langton the briefest outline he could regarding the Rome corruption case. He ended up with some pros and cons. Pro: somebody staged a professional-seeming hit on a person from Rome. The victim had some tenuous drug connections. There was the assault in jail, which might have been a failed attempt to keep Rodney from shooting off his mouth; and there was just a hint that another such assault might have happened, within the same circle of young people. The possible actor in those assaults had a Rome connection himself: he was in jail ostensibly for fleeing from the Rome cops. Con: Rodney was such an unassuming figure, it was hard to picture him knowing much of anything worth being killed over. And all the Rome connections could be wildly coincidental.

"When did you figure that out?" Jenn wanted to know.

"I guessed, and Doug more or less confirmed it by not stepping on me when I brought it up. That's why they're in this at all."

"But what was that about one side getting indicted and not the other?"

"Well," said Mac, "Corruption takes two. Somebody getting paid and somebody paying. And nobody on the paying side of that case seems to have been picked up. They're still running around out there."

"You think that's something Rodney knew about?"

"Beats me. We need to find out. And all I can think of is to see if we can find Robert Hagland."

For some reason, an ordinary Michigan farm town, originally called Tolanville, renamed itself after the Italian fashion city, Milan. Just as other Midwest towns with absurd pretensions have done (Marseilles, Illinois, comes to mind), Milan, or more accurately its residents and neighbors, got the pronunciation wrong: in Milan, Michigan, the accent is on the first syllable, not the last, and the 'i' is long. In fact, nothing about the place but the spelling suggests any connection with Europe at all, except the demographics. Of its six thousand citizens, almost ninety-three percent identify themselves as white folks.

Among those people were the family of Bobby Hagland, living outside the city to the east, on a smallish farm, backed up onto a Monroe county drain. In order to pay them a visit, Jenn Langton picked MacArthur up at his house at eight AM on Wednesday morning. Eight was normal starting time for her, hellishly early for Mac. In the gusting rain and wind, they drove through Mac's chosen triangle coffee shop, and Mac punched Hagland's parole address into his GPS. He propped it up on the dashboard of Jenn's car, and the nice lady's voice told them to take Washtenaw Avenue east to M-23 and then go south.

It's fifteen minutes or less down 23 to Milan, and if you exit and go east, away from the town, the countryside is instantly rural and agricultural. Between the highway and the Hagland house, there was nothing commercial at all except a tractor repair shop. The farmhouse itself was a frame building, showing the add-ons and generally organic growth that old homes on large amounts of land tend to. Trees hid part of it from the road, and a stack of firewood stood by the roadside, either for sale or just because. The driveway ran in beside the house and made a loop around a huge blue spruce tree.

Jenn parked her car squarely in the drive. It was a good thought, anyway, although if Hagland was here and decided to drive off, he could get by easily just by running over the lawn. Mac was pleased, though, to see Jenn doing anything tactical, so he said nothing about it. They went up to the door and knocked.

Bobby's father, Phillip Hagland, was a man about Mac's age or a bit more. He didn't seem surprised to have a visit from the police, and he wasn't in the least surprised that it was about his son. "Yeah," he said, "I thought you'd be comin' by to check on him."

"To check on him?" Jenn asked. "Check how?"

"About his parole, I mean."

"Oh, I see. I'm not a parole officer, though. I'm a detective, like I said, from Ann Arbor. We just want to ask him about ... well, about what he might have heard from his cell mate in jail."

"Oh," said Phil Hagland, and he sounded disappointed. "Well, unfortunately, he's not around."

"Do you know when he might be back?" asked Mac. "Or how we might get in touch with him?"

"Sorry to say, no, I don't," said the father, without sounding at all sorry. "He just left, what? Four days ago? Borrowed his brother's truck and drove off."

"Really? Four days ago?" said Mac.

"No idea where he might have gone?" added Jenn.

"Nope."

"Any other family he might have gone to see? Or friends? He isn't married, right?"

"Nope, no family here besides us. He's had girlfriends, I guess, but he doesn't talk about 'em. Some friends, too, but they don't come in and say 'hello', if you understand me."

"They don't?"

"No, if he was going somewhere with 'em, they'd just pick him up, sit out in the driveway and wait for him. But mostly, he'd go off on his own."

"And that's what he did this time?" Mac asked. "Went off by himself, in ... what did you tell me, his brother's truck?"

"Yeah, his brother's Chevy. They took his old Ford when he got arrested, but he's got keys to the Chevy."

"And how about his brother? Doesn't he need his truck back?"

"Not yet, no. He's in the army. In Afghanistan. Won't be back 'til the fall, probably."

"Does Robert have a cell phone?" asked Jenn. "Could we try calling him? Like I said, we're not after him, we just think he might have heard something that would help us out. With another, um, investigation."

"Mamie!" the old man yelled, directing his voice toward the back of the house. "Mamie! Do you know Bobby's cell number?"

Mrs. Hagland did not know the number by heart, but she had it written down someplace. While she looked for it, they determined that Bobby had been gone since the day before the murder probably took place. Neither parent had seen him go, and neither one really knew if he'd taken much of anything with him. Mamie Hagland came back with the cell phone number and the statement that a big basket of laundry, probably half the clothes Bobby owned, was still in his room. She couldn't say whether that meant he'd likely be back or likely not.

Jenn stepped to the front door and tried calling the cell. While she did, Mac brought up the truck again, obliquely, since it was the most obvious thing Bobby would have in his possession.

"So your other son's in Afghanistan? My nephew is over there, too. What's your boy's name? Maybe they know each other."

"Our other boy's Frank, Frank William. He's a private."

"Frank. Okay, I'll see. My nephew's a mail clerk, knows a lot of people. Maybe they've run into each other."

Phillip Hagland was about to say something about that when suddenly there was a loud, tinny noise coming up the basement stairs, a small and inexpensive speaker, playing a poor rendition of *Dixie.* It was Bobby Hagland's cell phone, responding to Jenn's call. The phone turned out to have been left lying on a lopsided dresser which otherwise held nothing of interest, including a few pairs of socks and boxers.

As they were leaving, Mac asked Dad what kind of Chevy Frank had. The old man said it was an S-10, the small one, with a cap. That kind of gold-beige color. Mac knew exactly what he meant by that; Chevrolet had sold many, many thousands of those little trucks, and many, many of them were painted that same innocuous color. Mac's own mother had driven one, in fact, and he knew two people with the same thing, one of them just down the street from his house. It wouldn't be a stand-out vehicle, not an easy one to spot.

Outside, the temperature had gone up enough to ensure that only rain, that is, water in its liquid, non-frozen state, was falling. Jenn ran for the car, Mac followed at his fastest pace, a kind of hasty walk. Everything ached, and he was wearing his detective clothes, not his warm and dry outfit. Jenn was about to back the car out, but Mac said, "No, go forward, around the back, around this driveway loop here. I want to see what's back there."

Behind the house, there was a single flat modern barn, a tractor-shed in fact, nothing like the red, hip-roofed image of 'barn' that urban kids think of when they think of farming. It was a place to store equipment, not produce nor animals. The doors were closed, and Mac assumed that if there were farm vehicles, or even Frank's gold-beige Chevy S-10 anywhere around, they'd be inside it. Bobby Hagland himself might be in there, waiting for the cops to leave. But he doubted it. It didn't seem as though this boy was all that popular with his folks. If they were afraid of him, maybe they'd lie for him, but simple familial affection didn't seem likely.

A large GMC pickup and an older Buick were parked out in the open: Dad's and Mom's cars, respectively. If Bobby had taken one of those, maybe the parents could be induced to report it as stolen, Mac thought. But with the brother's truck, it was still 'borrowing', at least for a while. The best he could think of was that Jenn would try to get the parole officer to violate the kid, and connect him with the Chevy. Then there'd be at least a vague chance that a cop, somewhere, would see it and have a reason to pull it over. If he or she didn't have something better to do. Cops in this budget-starved state didn't have a lot of spare time to read vehicle lists anymore.

"I didn't know you had a nephew," Jenn said.

"I don't. I just wanted the brother's name so we can get the Chevy's license plate."

Jenn turned out of the driveway and pointed the car back toward 23. "What now?" she asked Mac.

"You're in charge, lady," he said. "I think there's a bunch of phone calls to be made, though."

"Right. The parole officer," she said. "Who else?"

"Secretary of State. Find out a license plate number for the Chevy. Or just do it online. Then see if you can get the parole officer to put it out. Off-chance somebody'll see it. And I think I'd call the cops in Rome and Sturgis, too. Our friend was grabbed in Sturgis for a little bit of weed, but he went to jail for fleeing in Rome. What was that about? Who was the officer? That sort of thing."

"What would we get out of that?"

"Probably nothing much at all. But there might be a hint in it about whether he'd be going back to either place. Like in Rome, for example: did he run away from a house? If so, we might want to know the address, whose house it was, like that. Same thing in Sturgis. Just any old detail that might tell us where he is and what he's up to."

"Sturgis. Where is it, anyway?"

"Beats me. Somewhere out west past Jackson, I think."

"Okay, Mac," Jenn said. "You look a little rocky, though. Do you want to go home while I spam people?"

"Yes, please," said Mac. "I don't tend to be out and getting rained on quite this early, these days. I might lie down for a bit." He did, in fact, look bad, paler than usual. His right hand was clamped down hard on his knee, unconsciously trying to subdue the joint pain. He'd skipped his painkillers this morning because, technically, you weren't supposed to mix them with firearms. He was not going to poke around unarmed after someone who might be as Bobby Hagland might be. "That's another thing," he said. "See if you can find out whether Bobby has any guns."

While Mac stirred uneasily on his couch, Jenn Langton settled down to calling people and doing searches. She got the S-10's plate number and VIN easily enough, and after some delay, got a call back from Officer Dick Jastrimski, out in Rome. He described the contact with someone driving that truck, a truck that he'd contacted before. That sounded a bit thin to Langton, but she kept listening. The first time, Dick J. told her, the driver had been Robert Hagland. The second time, it had been Hagland on foot, going into a bar, and probably fleeing out the back of that bar, since a suspicious person had been seen and then the S-10 itself had also been seen, but had escaped.

"And that's it?" Jenn asked.

"Yes, that's what we have here."

"So no addresses? He wasn't at somebody's house or something?"

"No."

"Nobody with him? No passengers?"

"No." Jastrimski was beginning to sound a little defensive. He'd assured himself before returning Jenn's call that she was, in fact, a cop and not a lawyer, but even so, he knew that he had no proof that Bobby had fled from anything that evening – he might have been sitting in The Shed the whole time.

"Okay," Jenn said. "Well, we're just really poking around in the dark, here – we think we might, maybe, be interested in him for something bigger than usual, but it's sketchy so far. And we can't find him, either. So if you think of anything, call me."

"I will," Dick said, "But you can't find him? Isn't he in jail, still?"

"No, he got out a while ago. And he's not at home, at the address given, anyway."

"Well, bust him with his parole officer, at least. Tell me he's at least on parole?"

"Oh, yes. We're going that path, too. But it won't give us much unless someone spots him. And by the way, he's driving that S-10."

"Well, good. I'll keep an eye out for that," said Dick. "Anything else?"

Jenn thought over the call. Had she forgotten to ask anything? Probably, but she couldn't imagine how she'd ask a Rome patrol officer if anyone had arranged for Hagland to be jailed at the same time as Rodney Garfield, let alone put in the same cell. Not without bringing up topics she shouldn't. And Jastrimski hadn't even explained why the sight of Bobby going into a bar would automatically make him a suspicious individual. Suddenly, she found herself just a bit suspicious, too.

The call to the Sturgis PD was more pleasant, more chatty, and slightly more useful. The officer who'd caught Bobby picked up the phone almost at once, since he was just getting ready to start a shift. He explained that he'd pulled over himself to issue a parking ticket or at least make the driver of an old F-150 move his truck. But the man had run from him, dropping small amounts of marijuana, and had eventually surrendered. He would have gotten off with a misdemeanor, but then the fleeing thing in Rome had come up, and they handed him over to Wayne County. End of story.

"So what was he doing when he ran?" asked Jenn.

"Well, not clear, exactly, but I'd guess he was either buyin' or sellin' the dope. He was standing at the driver's window of another truck, something red."

"Any information on that?"

"No. Didn't even really get the make of the truck. Just red. By the time my backup rolled up, he was long gone. Or she. Just didn't get a look, I was runnin' so hard after your guy."

"He didn't have any weapons, did he?"

"No. Well, a little pocket knife, but no guns, no nukes, nothin' illegal."

"And you'd never seen him, Hagland, before?"

"Nope. If he hung out over here, we hadn't run into him."

"Did he seem to be running *to* someplace – a house or something?"

"We asked him why he ran, but he wouldn't say anything. He just ran down Main Street, left up Clay Street, you know, where the drug store is …"

"Sorry," said Jenn, "I've never actually been in Sturgis."

"Oh, too bad. Well, it's a side street. Back up there, then right down an alley and gave up. So, no, I guess I'd say he was just runnin', not trying to get somewhere. He doesn't have an address out here, does he?" He sounded mildly repelled at the thought of Bobby Hagland living in his jurisdiction.

"No, no," Jenn assured him, "He's from over here. Lives in Milan, down toward Toledo."

"Oh, good to hear it. I was afraid we'd missed something. You know he showed false ID at first?"

"What? No, I hadn't gotten that. He used a bogus name?"

"Yep. Hold on, I can tell you what it was. Here we go, Phil Wayne. Easy to spot as a false ID, too. Not a license or anything, just an employee ID from some car dealer. Looked like a photo copy, plastic coated."

"Really? You wouldn't know what dealer, would you?"

"Hmm … you know, it don't tell me, here in the report. I could go look in the evidence room, call you back."

"If you would, that would be great," said Jenn. "And let me give you the info on the truck we think he's driving now. If anybody spots him, he's off his parole."

"Okay, uh, Detective Langton, well I'll get back to you shortly, if I can run down that fake ID. And if we see that Chevy, we'll pick your fella up."

So, thought Jenn, *Hagland had fake ID when he was over there. But he didn't have it or didn't use it when the Rome cops stopped him the first time. Or they didn't say so*. What might that mean, if anything at all?

While Langton wondered about what people were and weren't telling her, Mac was lying down at home, but he didn't sleep at once. From the couch in his office, he could see up and out a window, toward the top branches of a tree. He remembered watching it in this same position last spring. Then it was fully leafed out and making an inverted cone of green against the sky; a fractal pattern if you accepted that pale mathematician's view of the universe, a perfect exposition of chaos otherwise. Back in the spring, it had held perfectly still for minutes at a time; next a gust of wind up there at fifty feet would toss the whole thing into movement, the wind pushing one way, the branches' elasticity pushing back, and all of it backlit in brilliant sunlight through the green leaves.

Mac couldn't go quite the whole way with the chaos theorists. He didn't believe that a butterfly could flap its wings in Tokyo and the Washington Monument would be blown over in DC. But he did sometimes think that if a really big butterfly in a nearer location, Des Moines, maybe, flapped very hard in the morning, and if a squirrel had made a bad choice about his home tree, by the afternoon, his nest might fall.

Today, there was no nest, and the branches were almost bare, just showing a hint of buds. The rain had stopped, leaving a damp gray world outside. On the floor, their old Shepherd twitched her hind legs and snuffled in her sleep. Mac closed his eyes, shifted his aching knees slightly, and drifted off to a dream of squirrels and bad choices.

Death's brother

> *One holds for earthlings the far-seeing light;*
> *The other holds Death's brother, Sleep, in her arms:*
> *Night the destroyer, shrouded in fog and mist.*

Michael Calley knew a great deal about a narrow range of things. He knew, for example, the key features of a good lie: most of it should be true, making the false part harder to identify. He knew the capabilities of many electro-mechanical-chemical devices, and how to maintain and modify them, and how to make sure they had the fuel or lubricants or ammunition required to keep them working. He knew nothing at all about post-modernism or quantum mechanics or women; the wines of south-western France were not part of his expertise. But movement of material from one place to another *was* a very strong suit for him, and in the later parts of his career, he'd done a certain amount of travel outside the US. If it had ever occurred to him or if there had ever been any random chance of falling into it, he might have made a good minor actor: people who met him usually considered him easy to know, and in fact, almost no one knew him at all, in any useful way.

When he told Uncle Peter DeVoos, sitting in that Rockford diner, about his background — military and defense and so on — he was telling the ninety percent true portion of a long and involved lie. In fact, he *had* been in the military, the US Army, for nearly twenty years. Almost of all of that time was spent in postings in the US or in protected rear areas overseas, doing jobs involving supply. Calley was not the guy with a bayonet, but the guy who made sure that those who needed bayonets had them. He didn't take any strategic objectives, but he took crates off transport aircraft and moved them onto trucks. Later, when he'd moved up through a series of non-commissioned officer ranks, he made sure that someone else moved the crates and that they were properly checked and accurately inventoried and delivered only to those who were supposed to have them.

That kind of career offered a number of distinct temptations, obviously. Many very expensive and, to Calley, intrinsically interesting kinds of goods passed through his hands. To the credit of the army's auditing and inspecting procedures, virtually none of the goods stuck to them: To Calley's hands, that is. Actual out-and-out fraud and theft were in fact rare in his branch of the army, and for reasons rooted in his personality, he himself was very, very clean in his dealings. He left the army, finally, as an E-6, a staff sergeant, with not quite twenty years of service, and a very unexceptional record: good, steady, undistinguished work. Up to that point, nothing anyone could easily discover about him would fall outside the bounds of an unexceptional life.

But Michael Calley (Mike to everyone who dealt with him) did not really have an unexceptional life. To begin with, he didn't grow up under ideal circumstances. The cover story, the carefully engineered lie he was now telling people when he had to, varied from reality in some important ways. For one thing, he was not from Sturgis, Michigan. The land he mentioned to Uncle Peter existed, and Calley did intend to buy it, but it was not his old family farm. It was someone else's old family farm, sitting vacant and for sale in a part of the state where farmland was not a gold mine, not a spot to develop a mall, not a site for a nice new gated community. Land booms have their limits, and not even the wildest-eyed developer had yet to put together a business plan for that particular part of the Michigan/Ohio border counties. Calley had a plan of his own.

He'd grown up in the home of his stepmother; his natural mother walked out on Dad after he broke her jaw for the second time. Dad remarried, got drunk one deer season evening, and died of hypothermia, passed out in a patch of woods in the Upper Peninsula. Dad and Stepmom hadn't had any additional children, but one of her sequence of post-widowhood boyfriends moved in for a while, bringing an older son of his own. This was when Mike was nine or ten, and he and the teenager shared a room and a bed. Calley never talked about what did or didn't happen, but he reached puberty himself with an absolute lack of interest in sex. Whether he was born a complete asexual or was made one, he never bothered to explore. He just kept his hands to himself, his pants zipped, and, metaphorically, his legs crossed. If someone noticed his single state or urged him to seek out a soul mate, he'd pass it off as lightly as the situation allowed. If anyone

92

made an issue of it, Calley withdrew from the acquaintance. After a while, everywhere he lived, everywhere the army posted him, his circle of friends became filtered to those who accepted him as a guy who'd have made a good monk.

When Calley got out of high school, he had no place to go, economically. He scored pretty well on standardized tests, in spite of the wretched quality of the public schools he attended. He had an aptitude for doing things according to a procedure, over and over again, until the procedure changed. Then he could adapt to it quickly and do things by the new procedure, over and over again, more or less without limit. He would not be the one to change the procedure; he would never lead a quality circle or run a kaizen event, but he would respond reliably, and he'd do things by whatever book was currently in use. The problem was, Michigan's Upper Peninsula didn't offer many jobs that required that sort of thing; manufacturing, for example, was not a word spoken up there often, nor was anyone hiring large numbers of clerks or QA people or staffers who lived and died by the checklist. In fact, nobody was really hiring anyone to do anything.

On the other hand, Mike was polite and reasonably fit. He'd dabbled in the two most solitary sports available in his schools: cross-country running and wrestling. Neither one was a path to popularity, but they kept off the cheeseburger poundage, and although our country's military recruiters hadn't yet begun to wake up at night screaming, as they contemplated the legions of pre-diabetic, obese teenagers who would be the next generation of US soldiers and sailors, it was already a known issue: the kids were out of shape. So when Mike, just turned eighteen and in pretty darn good shape, walked in the door, the army representative was ready to deal.

Basic training was what it always was: a sorting process. You got a label early on, and 'combat' was never a label anyone applied readily to Mike. He looked like a form-filler and he acted like one, and as soon as he got to do anything useful for the army, he demonstrated a high level of skill at form-filling. But in the army, even a form-filler was a warrior of a kind, living in a society where everybody was hypothetically proficient with a firearm.

In the rural parts of Michigan, as in a number of other US states, a substantial part of the population are raised in the presence of guns, bows, and hunting. It's part of the culture. The few fall weeks of deer season and the two separate turkey hunts are almost on a par with saints' days. They have rituals, pilgrimages, special raiment, family events. Kids are given guns for birthdays or Christmas early in their lives, and they learn rudimentary rules of safety and usage in much the same way they learn to drive; with Dad or an older brother or Uncle Fred, out in the woods or in the cornfield. These people aren't gun nuts or rabid extremists or uniformed militia members; they're just who the rural lower middle class are in the Midwest: people who understand firearms. Mike was part of that from before he enlisted, and now he was living in an armed society, doing essentially the job of the armorer in a feudal world: others used the weapons, perhaps, but he made them or bought them or fixed them or handed them out.

The more he did that job, the more he learned about the industry and the technology. Everyone he saw on a daily basis had or could potentially have one of the most admired personal weapons in the history of individual combat: an M-16. Eventually, as his career and rank grew, tens of thousands of M-16 rifles passed across his desk, literally or on paper. Beside the M-16s, there was explosive ordinance, machine guns, ammunition in almost unimaginable quantities, body armor, exotic sighting equipment, everything that the Pentagon felt its troops ought to have, right down to the proverbial pointed stick. It was all Mike's concern.

In the course of that, there'd been a few unsettling incidents. Other soldiers or even a civilian would spend a few evenings at a bar, trying to get to know Mike. None of these people were ever very subtle or even particularly smart, and it didn't take long to see what the sub-text was. Mike never bit — he always played dumb, with a kind of Nixonian "Yes, but that would be illegal" response. But he never forgot even the smallest details of the propositions which were, after all, quite simple: money in return for hardware. He might have felt differently if he hadn't been close to another NCO, not quite so cautious. That individual, from another unit stationed with Mike's, made a few thousand dollars off a handful of select-fire receivers, the parts that would turn a semi-auto civilian rifle into a very illegal, full-automatic weapon. Then, since neither party to the deal was especially smart nor even remotely trustworthy, the sergeant got fifteen years in the United States Disciplinary Barracks at Fort Leavenworth. Everyone else on the base got lectured about it extensively if non-publicly, and those with any actual opportunity to do similar deals came under intense scrutiny from above.

Calley took it all very much to heart. It was oppressive enough, in fact, that he took a transfer overseas to get away from the atmosphere, and it colored his point of view about fighting city hall, bucking the system, sticking his neck out, and a whole list of other euphemisms for not stepping out of line.

It did not, though, change his interest in military technology. Very early on, as soon as he had the spare thousand dollars or so that it took, he'd bought himself a very good example of a civilian AR-15, a legal, semi-automatic version of the army's standard weapon. It chambered the same cartridge, it looked very much the same, and the only important technical difference was that instead of continuing to fire when you held the trigger down, it only fired once for each time you moved your finger. That's what semi-automatic meant. Like the M-16 whose sibling they are, ARs were designed to be upgradable, with all kinds of fascinating gear to add on: laser sights, high-powered flashlights, special single-point slings. Owning one didn't make you a combat infantryman, but it was as close as Mike wanted to be.

And once you had an AR or something like it, there were other guns and equipment on which to spend your pay. By the time Mike sat down one evening in a German bar, near the Hohenfels Training Area, his collection, all in storage back in the states, was fairly large if all completely legal. Even his foreign-made guns, if he modified them at all, were in compliance with an obscure US law regarding how many of the upgrade parts were made in which country. Again, he was good at following procedures. But this time, the fellow who sat down with him wasn't offering any kind of off-the-record deal. He was, in fact, a personnel agent, talking to as many overseas American NCOs as he could on a two-week trip. He worked for a large and, at that point, little known company, one that was involved with defense contracting of an old, old kind; not quite as old a career as prostitution, but nearly. The modern euphemism was 'security', but what it amounted to was soldiers for hire: mercenary services.

Now, Mike was obviously not the *Soldier of Fortune* magazine type, something even a civilian recruiter could tell, just from his insignia. But mercenaries of any kind, over or under the counter, needed smart supply people almost as much and sometimes more than they did ordinary shooters. In fact, combat *per se* was something the military tended to reserve unto itself. Just short of actual offensive operations, though, there were contractors all over the globe, manning gates, riding shotgun in convoys, keeping diplomats and more exalted contractors from being kidnapped or simply assassinated. And that was only the work done for the uniformed branches; other government agencies needed muscle, too, as did corporations, foreign governments, and even less official organizations. It was, in fact, the beginning of a boom in private security, and experienced bodies were in demand. The one law that everyone was obeying, no matter how much attention they paid to others, was that of supply and demand.

At first, Mike didn't understand the difference between this pitch and the ones he'd heard before. But it sunk in quickly that what was being offered was a job, not a crime, and a job with a much larger pay package than he was getting. He was astounded at the whole thing. He'd heard about people quitting and going with contractors, but it had never occurred to him that he'd get an offer. He'd hung on in the army mostly through not having any ideas or ambitions about something different, and the difference here was that he didn't have to imagine it, visualize it, research it, apply for it, network for it, pass a test, or do anything else: all he had to do was accept it, start going to work in civilian clothes, and make more money.

He thought about it for forty-eight hours and said "Yes." The recruiter helped him with the paperwork (all in a day's work for a good Human Resources man), and as quickly as was possible, Mike was US Army, retired and a new employee of Northern Sector Consulting, a meaningless name, deliberately designed to obscure the sort of work being done. They were good at what they did and efficient in other ways, too. It took them less than five years to fully develop the sociopath in Mike Calley.

At first, things seemed as advertised. He made nearly twice as much in salary as he had in the army, and they kept him in the US, mostly in their Arizona office. He worked under the direction of other people, and as far as he knew, nothing he did was illegal. Primarily, he bought things and had them shipped to various places. He was very good at this, but it was an unexceptional set of skills, and not many people at Northern Sector paid much attention to him. Then a shipment of what was supposed to be NATO standard 5.56 millimeter rifle ammunition came in, from a new vendor that Calley had been instructed to use. By the merest chance, Mike decided to sample a bit, although Northern's contract to supply it didn't call for acceptance testing. Mike had heard a thing or two, however, about the customer, a vicious set of bastards who were the management of a well-funded security agency in a small Middle-Eastern country; he suddenly and uncharacteristically developed a paranoid feeling about springing this new supply stream on them, sight unseen. So he opened a case or two, took out a box from each at random, and drove over to a local rifle range. His personal AR-15 was always in his car, carefully cased up, and he planned on putting a few of these east-Europe-sourced rounds through it, just to ease his conscience.

The first round failed to fire. Mike's rifle was always in top condition; this couldn't, he thought, be a mechanical failure. He waited sixty seconds with the gun pointed safely downrange, ejected the cartridge and looked it over; there was a clear firing pin dent in the primer. He picked the rifle back up and chambered another round: same result. Out of forty cartridges, not one went off, and when he broke out his combination tool and pulled out one of the bullets, the reason was clear. The propellant looked like no gun powder he'd ever seen. In fact, it looked like sand. In fact, it was. And the primers were just little metallic-colored plastic disks, without any explosive medium, either.

As a younger and less experienced person, Mike might have gone straight back to the office and blown the whistle. Today, though, he stopped in his tracks, mentally, and started thinking through possibilities. Simple QA statistics told him that the whole shipment was bogus. A hundred-percent bad outcome of a random sample was good enough for him on that score. The important question was: what to do about it? His immediate superior had given him this supplier and directed him to buy from them. This would not make his boss look good, especially when the Minister of Assassination at the client agency received twenty thousand rounds of useless ammunition and started making phone calls. If Mike said nothing, the outcome would be negative for Northern, his boss, and probably for him, too. If his boss already knew about the problem — if he'd been incentivized, shall we say, by the supplier to accept and ship this rubbish — then he'd need someone to blame it on, and that could well be Mike.

Given his usually methodical way of thinking, it took Mike a surprisingly short time to analyze the various risks and decide on his next step. He concluded that what he needed to do was spread things around, preferably in an upward direction. If he could have, he'd have called a meeting with the head of the company, but he didn't have that kind of access. What he could do, he realized, was simultaneously tell both his boss, Peter, and Peter's boss, the head of the Arizona operation. That person was a tall, cold woman named Elizabeth who had retired from the army as a captain. Liz was considered capable if harsh, and she was Peter's immediate superior. Telling them both at the same time would keep Peter from sticking Mike with it, at least. And If Liz was on the wrong side of this too and fired him, well, that would be just too bad. It was as much risk mitigation as he could think of, given that the stuff was supposed to ship tomorrow.

It took less than an hour to make it happen. The three of them met in a second-floor conference room, and Mike explained what he'd discovered. He finished up by pulling a couple of additional rounds apart, demonstrating their quality shortcomings. Peter made a good show of being furious with the supplier, Liz said very little, and in about ten minutes, Mike was asked to go back to his desk and wait for further instructions. As he walked back downstairs, he checked his watch; he estimated that in half an hour or so, he'd know if he still had a job.

In fact, it took far less than that. He'd only just sat down when his phone rang, and he was asked to come back up. This time, Peter was not present, and Liz was in the conference room with a young new employee; she asked Mike to take this additional headcount with him, go back to the warehouse, and do as much testing as he considered necessary to prove that the whole shipment was bad. He was to take as much time as needed, as long as it wasn't more than forty-eight hours. He was to report the outcome to her, in person, and neither of them was to talk about it otherwise. And she would talk to the customer about an unfortunate delay in shipping.

Mike said, "Yes, Ma'am," and just stopped himself from saluting. "And you know, we have almost this much known-good product from the previous vendor ..."

"That was going to be my next question," she said. "Put a hold on it, in case we have to ship."

Peter was not heard from again; he took a new job with one of the larger aerospace companies. Mike stayed with the Scottsdale office for a while longer, reporting directly to Liz. His confidence improved; he broke his apartment lease and bought a small house. He upgraded his vehicle, buying an Explorer. And he bought some more hardware of the kind that interested him; for the first time, he bought a gun that wasn't strictly kosher, either in its nature or its origins. At a glance, it was just another Chinese assault rifle, legal enough if not inappropriately modified. But in fact, it was a brand new, full-auto-capable Czech-made weapon, provided for a small consideration to Mike by a seller who wanted to sell Northern several hundred of them. Mike bought the gun, took it out to the desert to fire a few times, then put it in storage with the rest of his gear, since he suddenly found himself promoted and on his way to Africa.

It happened very quickly. Liz called him in, waved him into a chair, and commenced one of her briefing-style conversations. They were typically one-way communications, designed to provide exactly the necessary amount of information, with spaces for questions, if any. Some of the staff disliked this style; they wanted a chattier boss. Mike preferred it. He liked clear directions and unambiguous objectives.

"Mike," Liz said, "you got out of the army at E6, so you had management responsibilities, you had people under you. Since you've been here, you haven't had that, but we want to give you some more advanced tasks. You want that?"

"Okay," Calley said. "I'd like to take a shot at it."

"Well, it's going to have to be more than a shot. This is going to call for three things from you. One, initiative. You're going to set up an on-site operation and make a lot of decisions for yourself. Two, you'll have people to manage. Three, you'll have security concerns. And there's not going to be room for screwing up. Any of that change your mind?"

"No, Liz, I don't think so. I'd like to do it." Calley had finally managed to stop calling her Ma'am.

"Okay, here's the outline. This is written up, too, and the first thing for you to do is flesh it out into an operation plan, but this is the executive summary. East Africa. Specifically Sudan. There're a lot of people doing a lot of fighting, and we have a logistics customer. But there are some issues with their funding, with how regularly they get it, that is. And we're concerned enough about that to take special measures, cash and carry, if you understand me."

"We don't deliver unless we're paid first?"

"Exactly. And paid in cash, US dollars or Euros. If the customer hands you a five, you give him five dollars' worth of product, just like buying gas used to be. And does that suggest why you might have a security issue?"

"Lots of cash on hand?"

"Right. And your operation is going to be in a sketchy place. Addis Ababa, in fact."

"Ethiopia?"

"Right again. Better than being in Sudan. But not a great neighborhood. You'll have four people with you. Three inventory guys and an accountant. All of them security-capable, with experience."

Calley knew that the phrase 'with experience' meant combat or at least close exposure to it. It meant that the inventory guys would move crates around and drive vehicles, but they'd also be armed and adept in using arms. The accountant, he assumed, would be a spy from the company, probably in direct touch with Liz, there to look over his shoulder.

"Any questions so far?" Liz asked.

"Sure. Let's see; who do I report to?"

"Me."

"Great. What's the total scope of service? Just supply or delivery, too?"

"You get the goods into Ethiopia. You hand 'em over to the customer, upon payment. He gets 'em out. You don't care how he does it, once it's on his vehicles. In fact, you aggressively don't know how he does it. Or if he gets them out at all."

"And the product is?"

"Mostly seven sixty-two by thirty-nine. Some explosives. Some RPG rounds. And occasionally, the guns themselves. Maybe some rations, clothing, first aid gear, too. But mostly munitions."

"Coming from where?" Seven sixty-two by thirty-nine was the caliber of the world-standard Russian-designed AK-47 assault rifle. Some general somewhere had said, "If you know how to use a shovel, in eight hours I can teach you to use an AK."

"East bloc, as usual," said Liz. "They like it over there, they're used to it."

"Quality?"

"Run of the mill. It feeds, it fits in the chamber. You pull the trigger, it goes off. That's good enough for these guys."

"Purchasing?"

"We'll do the sourcing, you order through here. You're in charge of quantities. So you need to keep up with what the customer will want on, say, a thirty-day basis. It'll take basically that long to get stuff to you."

"Okay," said Mike. "Communications?"

"Email for routine, HR stuff, admin. Secure sat phone for orders, financials, and anything sensitive. Anything about the customer, for example."

"How soon do we start?"

"Soon," said Liz. "You've got about two weeks here, still. Work out your plan, interview your guys. The deal is ninety-nine percent done now. It'll close in days, unless something happens. Then, you and Phil – you know Phil?"

Calley did know Phil. Was he going to be the accountant? Phil was Liz's financial analyst, reporting to Northern's CFO and working the Arizona division's numbers. If Phil was going, there was a question about how much in charge he, Calley, would be. And the contract was a bigger deal than it sounded like.

"Sure, I know Phil. Is he helping kick off, or is he assigned?"

"Phil? He'd quit if we made him move overseas. No, he's just going to help you with the regulations. The officials. You need a title over there, and he's got one. But you've got him for a week, tops. He'll give you your numbers person, though. Somebody from his team or somebody new, if he can hire fast enough." Liz glanced at her watch, and Mike caught the signal.

"Okay, I think I've got the picture. Two more questions: who do I hand over to here, and how big is the contract?"

"One, you hand off to Kathy, and two, it's a little weird, but it works out to a not-to-exceed of ten million a year, with year to year renewals. So your job is to make it worth ten million in the first year and keep it going for as many more as you can. But Mike, frankly, I'll take one year. That's about how long I expect the customer to stay employed. Anything longer than that is fine but not in my projections."

"So then I have another question: what about account development? I set up a depot and import procedures. What if I can find somebody else who needs that?"

"You can try, but you hand 'em off to me to negotiate. No free-lancing. If something comes in, you get a cookie, for sure. But you're not in a Business Development job. And we do have some not-talking-to-the-competition language in the contract. There'll be groups over there that are off-limits as long as we have the original deal."

"All right. I'll get started."

"Thanks. I backed you for this job, by the way. It's stuff you know how to do." Liz paused. "Oh, and I meant to show you this." She took a folded newspaper from her desk drawer. The second page was on top, with a headline circled, but it was meaningless to Mike. He could recognize Russian, but not read it. He looked up at Liz.

"It says, 'Belarus: Unlicensed Munitions Factory Explodes, Burns. Arson Suspected'."

To Make Boys Into Men

And she bore as well a holy brood of daughters
Who work with Apollo and with the Rivers
To make boys into men.

Mike's 'farm in Sturgis' wasn't actually in Sturgis. A place called Nottawa was closer by a couple of miles, but since Nottawa consisted of a chain of lakes, some houses and a lumberyard, Sturgis was the nearby town, and Sturgis being on US 12, there was genuine traffic, there were businesses, places to get a sandwich. Five miles north of Sturgis, up Michigan Highway 66 (motto: 'Not *That* Route 66') was an east/west county two-lane, and a mile down that was the farm.

Mike's place was a clever choice for the business plan he had in mind. The road was just well enough travelled that a convenience store might believably have a chance of surviving as long as it didn't try to make anybody rich, and there was absolutely nowhere else to buy a cup of coffee or a stale donut for miles. The guys and girls driving by to hook up with 66 and go up to their jobs in Battle Creek or Kalamazoo or Grand Rapids or else go south to 12 and on west to Indiana and even Illinois — those poor damn road warriors could start out with cheap caffeine and sugar from Mike's little front organization.

But it was the non-public aspects of the property that really made it attractive. First of all, it had a big footprint; it was a hundred and twenty acres, north and south of the road, with a blend of plowed corn field and second growth woods. It was not only a place to operate inconspicuously, it was a place you could get away from if you had to. On the south side of the road, the fields were in the middle, but both east and west borders were covered with woods, and a drain bisected the field, lined with just enough trees to provide cover. Near the southern end, a power line route had been cleared, then never used. It angled back northeast, running across a gravel north/south road, cross-country again through woods and a neighbor's field, and finally back to the two-lane. Although you

105

could only stay concealed going south if you were on foot, a reasonable four-wheel-drive vehicle could still get out and away quickly and then offer a choice of escape to either the west or the east.

To the north the evasion possibilities became even more interesting. Just a hundred and fifty yards out the back door of the barn, there was a wooded streambed that extended in an almost unbroken northwest line for three and half miles, right up to the back door of the last farmhouse on the southern edge of Nottawa. And in the pole barn belonging to that house, Calley had paid, under a different name, to store an aging Toyota Camry. If he had to, he could take a three or four hour walk in the woods, let himself into the barn and the car, and camp until the roadblocks came down, then drive away. It might not be foolproof, but in the middle of the heartland of a fully developed nation, it wasn't too bad an escape plan.

Of course, that was all worst-case planning. The operational aspects were good, too. As-is, the farm provided a large if somewhat rundown house and an even larger barn. And there was ample room for a store between the barn and the road. Behind the house, there were sheds and random outbuildings, none in good enough condition to keep; they'd come down, but the house and the barn would be crucial. There were enough rooms in the house that accommodations for visiting customers and vendors wouldn't be a problem; there'd be no Sturgis motel bills to clutter up someone's credit card records, for example. And of course the barn would be both a warehouse and perhaps a production facility.

Gene DeVoos was actually reading job listings when Calley called him. The boy didn't have the slightest idea how to start a company, beyond having picked a name and ordered magnetic signs for his truck, and he hadn't lined up any business at all. This polite stranger on the phone who mentioned his uncle Peter and seemed to have a plan and a site and some assets was a *deus ex machina* for Gene; it would have taken an older, wiser head to see anything more than kindly fate in what was being suggested.

The initial elements of it were simple, a bigger job than Gene had expected to get but nothing so far outside his existing world that it would scare him off. This Mr. Calley was going to start up a small business down by Sturgis, and he needed someone to help him put up a convenience store, fix up some existing buildings, and then, maybe, go on to some other things. He said he didn't like having to find someone new for each new task. He'd rather have one guy, like Gene, kind of on staff. He gave Gene an address, a PO box in Sturgis, and asked him to send a resume.

With some help from an old high school teacher, Gene put together a small masterpiece, carefully and only slightly exaggerating each of the construction jobs and general areas of knowledge he could come up with. At the last minute, it occurred to him to parlay his one-time experience with reading Clay's sermon into 'Assistant Pastor' at the Farmer's First Community. He was reasonably literate and also willing to take advice on something like this, and the teacher didn't question the facts, knowing nothing at all about Clay DeVoos except his lurid death. He just did a little editing and handed it back. What Gene ended up mailing to Mike Calley described a mature-sounding and respectable individual.

When Mike read it over, most of it sounded fine and some of it gave him a bit of concern. The person he really wanted was someone currently clean but corruptible. 'Assistant Pastor?' Would this DeVoos fellow be *too* clean? And if so, could he be utilized just for the overt aspects of the business? How much trouble would it be to keep the other side of things out of sight? He thought it over for a day, and then decided he'd need to talk to the candidate. He called Gene, said nice things about the resume, and set up a meeting at a restaurant in Kalamazoo, reasonably close to the half-way point between Sturgis and Grand Rapids.

When they met, in a chain restaurant just off I-94, Mike saw a young man, a little younger-looking than he'd expected, with a reserved and respectful affect. It reminded him of new soldiers, not long out of basic training, and that was good for Gene's cause, since it was essentially what Calley wanted: someone with a small amount of general qualification and not too much ambition and attitude.

They talked about backgrounds. Calley gave him the standard, edited brief on what he, himself, had done in life, and in return, got Gene's carefully constructed take on his own situation. His father was dead, murdered in cold blood for inexplicable reasons, and his mother struggling with a nervous breakdown. This was delivered without drama; Gene could be very deadpan when he wanted to. He'd thought this over on the drive down, and debated how a stranger and potential employer would react. Just concealing the facts didn't seem like a very good idea. He thought it would be worse, later on, to have a boss find out the details than to just state them up front. What he didn't know about Calley, of course, was that he was almost as parentless a man, himself. Mike saw it as weird, a bit, that a real estate client had blown Clay DeVoos' head off, but not a disqualifying characteristic for the son. His own father's death, after all, had been self-inflicted, and he hadn't spoken to his mother in twenty-five years. So with a few polite expressions of sympathy, he let that aspect of the interview drop.

They talked about the work to be done, designing and building a simple store front, a place that would inventory mostly packaged goods, a small amount of perishables, beer and wine when they could get a license. A coffee station, of course. There'd need to be space for lottery-tickets, connections for an ATM and credit card processing. Calley had done just enough of the leg work so far that he'd ruled out selling gasoline; the zoning variance to do retail was one thing, but putting in storage tanks was more of a commitment than he wanted to take on. This led them into a discussion of legalistics and licenses, and it went from there to franchising. Mike's initial thought, when he'd begun putting this all together, had been to go that way, let someone else deal with supply and branding and advertising. But the more he worked over the details, the less he liked the idea of having a corporate entity poking around. They wanted more traffic than the road could supply. They wanted to come and inspect things. They had distinct ideas about image and turnover and, especially, profit margins; none of that matched what Calley had in mind himself: a front business that would usually show a loss or at best a small profit and absorb attention from other things that would be going on in the buildings out back.

He didn't put it that way to Gene, but he did have some critical comments about big companies, and that seemed to hit a sore spot with the boy. His expression changed, and he looked down at the table. "I agree with that, Mr. Calley," he said. "You know, I never really believed that old farmer was just crazy. There were some big real estate people in that deal ..." He let it tail off.

Interesting, thought Mike. *Very interesting. Could that be a hint of rebellion there? Could we, somewhere down the line, nudge that line of thinking into a willingness to ignore a federal law or two? Possibly.*

The outcome was that Mike offered Gene a job, initially on a contract basis, as Operations Manager. Gene would move down to Sturgis, Calley'd find him an apartment or something to rent, and they'd get things under way. There was mutual acknowledgement that neither of them was an expert on retail, but also a sense that it couldn't be rocket science. Mike smiled when he used that phrase, and it was a long time later on before Gene realized why.

The purchase of the farm had been nearly done already. Mike closed on it, took possession, and moved into the existing house. They confirmed that the open spot west of the house and in front of the barn would work, legally, for the store. It took months to get things unstuck with the zoning people, but they carried on with the parts of the deal that didn't involve a lot of unrecoverable spending. They talked to wholesalers, collected phone numbers, scribbled names for the store on napkins, having breakfast at what became their regular diner. From the owner, they got a recommendation on a self-employed book keeper. A lawyer in Virginia, who regularly handled things of quite another nature for Calley, dug around and found them a not-too-bright but moderately efficient attorney for local, routine matters. Calley told Gene he'd picked the guy out of the phone book. He didn't mention the man in Virginia.

Like a lot of old farm properties, this one had a scattering of odd, old structures. While Gene worked on the store and its complications, Mike rounded up a couple of local high school students and tore down what had been a chicken coop, something that might once have been a granary, and another shed whose original purpose was indeterminate. Then he rented a Bobcat with a blade and scraped out a much bigger gravel lot and driveway between the house and the barn. He told Gene that since there was no garage, he wanted to use the barn for his SUV.

By mid-summer, the store was ready, waiting on final inspections. Mike had a couple of young folks lined up to work the counter and stock shelves, and he was giving Gene an introduction-to-purchasing course. While the building and outfitting work had been going on, the two of them had evolved an understanding that there was another enterprise coming along after this one, nature unspecified, so far, but Mike made sure Gene knew he was neither out of a job nor stuck with running a convenience store.

When the county told them it would be another week before they could finish up the permits, Gene asked for the intervening time off. He went west to the shore, stayed in a motel, and logged time on the Lake Michigan beaches. For his age and experience, he was being paid well, and he was pleased with life. He did wonder what was going to happen next, but so far, Mike Calley had been a good boss, happy with progress, tolerant of delay and minor mistakes. That there was something else going on, perhaps not completely above board, had been clear for a while now. For example, there was the fact that Mike never went anywhere without a fairly obvious handgun under his jacket. Another was the habit Calley had of looking carefully around parking lots, especially in places they went often, before driving off. It didn't add up to Al Qaida-in-Michigan, but it was enough to let Gene speculate and decide what his reaction to it would be, when it surfaced. And the conclusion he came to was: ride the tiger.

While Gene was away, Mike called in a veteran he'd met informally, in the VFW hall of another town, as far away from the farm as was practical. This person was unemployed and in need of a job, and Mike used him to help with a project in the barn, one that he hesitated, still, to let Gene in on. It involved unloading an order of steel shelving from a truck, one that arrived after dark, and over the next few days, assembling the shelves around the inside walls of the barn. This worked out all right, but when it was done and the vet paid off, Mike could see that it wouldn't be reasonable to keep on using this kind of random, unverified help. Each new person who had anything to do with the second business was a security gap — this latest guy, for example, would go back to the VFW bar and tell somebody about his temporary job. Someone else who was out of work would get a ride with yet another somebody down to Sturgis, and drop in to see if there was any more work available. Then, there'd be three people more than there needed to be who knew about an old barn with things stored in it. And so on and so on.

So it would have to be Gene. Originally, Calley had thought he'd pull in another person, maybe someone he knew from the army or from the contractor world. But the more he thought about that, the less he could come up with anyone he trusted enough or who would trust him. Now it was time to get started on Business 2, and there wasn't anybody on tap who was a better bet than Gene DeVoos. So he sat down the evening before Gene was due back, wrote out a pitch in long hand, read it over two or three times, and then shredded the manuscript.

They sat down across the nice new desk in the store's office, and Mike introduced the topic of what came next. Gene had partly expected it to come up this morning, and he adopted the completely-absorbed expression he used whenever Calley was teaching him something.

It reminded him of the day his father had announced the church scheme. His reaction was surprise, then dismay, and then, this time, insight and disbelief, because what Calley was describing was preposterous. He told Gene that he was not actually ex-military but still in. In Intelligence, in fact, working to identify foreign groups that were illegally obtaining US technology. The money for this farm and the store and the rest was actually tax dollars at work. The object was to talk to the 'outsiders', as Calley called them, offer them merchandise, actually have some of it here to show them if necessary, and get as much information about them as they could. Anything after that would be handled by others, Mike said, and ...

Gene raised his hand. "Mike, hold on a minute."

"Okay," said Calley. "What?"

"You and I've known each other for a while now. I never thought you were just going to open a snack shop."

"Yeah? You were right about that."

"But, really ... I don't think this has anything to do with the government."

Mike's expression became as neutral as he could make it. "Okay, Gene ... you're going to have to tell me what you mean by that."

"I did some thinking when my father was killed. And I did more of it since then. I think you have to look out for yourself. Which Dad always tried to do. But you have to know that ... other people are doing that, too. Working for themselves. And he missed that. He thought everybody else would follow the rules, so if he didn't, he'd have an advantage."

"So ... what do you mean? You mean I'm looking out for myself, here? Not you?"

"What I mean is ... see if this makes sense to you. I don't think it's necessarily smart to always follow the rules, as long as it isn't stupid. Smoking crack and breaking into houses is stupid. Making money and employing people and, oh, buying cars and building the economy up isn't stupid. That's business, and I think both you and I know that business ... it doesn't always follow the rules."

"Ah," said Mike. "I remember a conversation we had about salesmen."

"Yeah, I was thinking about that."

"Where I said you have to have your bullshit detector turned on. And I think maybe yours is working pretty well, this morning."

"I didn't say that. But, sir, Mr. Calley, Mike ... I'm having a hard time with the explanation you just gave me."

Calley let out a breath. "Well, good. Because it *was* bullshit. And I apologize. Can I start over?"

"Sure."

"Well. It's ... simple and complicated, all at once. It's about supplying a demand. It has to do with the business I used to be in. And some of the people I used to know. It does actually run counter to the 'rules', I think you said. It makes a lot of money. You've heard that thing somebody said, about what governments spend their money on, guns or butter? This is guns."

It had been guns for Mike Calley for a long time. He'd handled arms for the army and for Northern Consulting, now he was going to handle them on his own account. The assets for a business that trafficked in weapons and ammunition and ancillary equipment were elemental: knowledge of the ways in which supply and demand could be coupled together and capital to acquire inventory. Credit was not so important, at least in the opening stages. Money, actual cash in hand, was everything. And Mike had some money, thanks to six or seven young idiots in Addis Ababa.

When Northern sent him to Ethiopia, he spent almost all his time learning the task at hand. There were few temptations for him and almost nothing to do except become very good at the job he'd been given. He and Phil, the financial guy from the company, smoothed the way effectively with the Ethiopian officials to the extent that he had very little to worry about with the import of his products. A cargo plane would land, well after dark, at Bole Airport. Mike and his team would be there, along with local drivers and trucks and some national police. There'd be a quick transfer of material and a short drive back to the facility. People on the streets, if any, wouldn't look too long or too carefully at the convoy as it went by.

Delivery, as Liz had stated, was a matter of taking payment and getting the goods onto a buyer's transport. When they drove out the gate at the back of Mike's depot, they ceased to exist, as far as he was concerned. Cash was accounted for and locked in a large safe. Periodically, it went from Addis to Turin by a company courier, and from there ... well, it went somewhere, and it was eventually credited to Liz's revenue report for the period. Northern had found a bright young Irish guy, Liam, to do the books for Mike, and they got along well. The other three staffers were Americans, two ex-army and one ex-cop, and they were primarily muscle. It wasn't an especially demanding assignment, nor was it all that exciting, but Mike enjoyed it. It was as close to an actual front-line job as he'd ever had.

Contrary to Liz's estimate, the customer didn't dry up after the first year. In fact, as the situation between the North and the South in Sudan got worse, the demand and the available funds actually increased. Mike had the operational procedures tuned almost to perfection, and it's hard to say how long the contract could have continued in his hands if that had been all that was required. There was a problem, though, with security.

If Mike had had any prior experience with running a business in a bad neighborhood, he might have avoided trouble, but it never occurred to him that the comings and goings of several Americans and of some well-dressed and well-equipped Sudanese would attract the attention of plain old street criminals. From having been a relatively safe city, as East African cities go, Addis was just beginning to see an upswing in mildly violent petty crime, and some of the area's dumber and poorer young men had noticed that something prosperous was going on behind the walls of Mike's building. So one evening, as two of the Northern Consulting staff guys were coming home on foot, three locals approached them and demanded money.

As it turned out, they'd made a colossal underestimate of the Americans. The street boys found themselves instantly at gunpoint, then knocked to the ground, kicked and beaten, and sent running off into the night without the two small knives and a stick they'd brought with them. It cured them of their ambition completely, but it didn't keep them from talking about it. And some of the people they talked to listened carefully.

In hindsight, Mike should have had a regular scheme for relocating the depot or having several sites and rotating among them. But the place he had was convenient to the airport, and it had been secure, so far. He was aware that the streets weren't safe, but his people had dealt with this first minor event very effectively. He ignored it.

That week, the big safe held nearly a million US dollars in cash. A courier was due on Friday to take it away, but on Wednesday, the customer called and placed a huge new order, unplanned for, that would amount to more than two and a half million Euros worth of rifles and ammunition. The purchasing agent wanted to bring the money to Mike immediately, since the longer he held on to that kind of cash, the more nervous he became. His superiors were not a very trusting set of people.

Mike was willing to receive the payment, but he pointed out that he had nothing like that kind of inventory on hand. He'd have to order it, and it might take a month to arrive. The buyer was fine with that — he had no transport lined up yet, anyway — but he still wanted to get the money off his hands. Mike agreed to take it, and they set up a time the next day, Thursday. The whole amount could go off with the courier on Friday, and all would be well.

Receipt of a big payment was an all-hands operation at the depot, and all three of the staff plus Liam the accountant were in the back of the building, in positions around the gates to the yard. However, instead of a car pulling up in the rear, there was hammering on the small, heavily locked front door. Only Mike, sitting in the office, was in a position to even hear it, and he looked out very carefully through a peep hole. His customer contact was outside, unaccountably having decided that it was safer or quicker or something to violate all agreed-upon procedures and just have his driver park on the street out front. Mike was not happy about this at all, but he unlocked the door, took the briefcase the man handed him, and gave him a blank receipt form along with a strong suggestion that he get the hell out of there. The buyer was only too willing, and he was out of sight in less than a minute.

Mike locked the door and went back to the office. He opened the safe, put the briefcase in, and relocked it. As he headed to the back of the building to find Liam and stand down the security boys, there was a loud metallic-mechanical crash, followed instantly by gunfire.

The word that had gotten around after the young thugs' fiasco that started out as, "Some bad dudes in that place." But like a game of telephone, it evolved to an idea that, yes, the Americans were armed and mean, but there were only two of them and, being Americans, they were exceedingly wealthy. This piece of intelligence, in the minds of an embryonic gang, became the centerpiece of a plan.

It was never clear, later, exactly how many of them there were, but by coincidence, this group of slightly-better-equipped criminals, all Ethiopian nationals from the city, chose this particular day to try a raid on Mike's shop. They were not an experienced crew; their tactical concept consisted of smashing through the back gates with a truck, firing their assortment of guns at whatever they found, and then becoming wildly rich on the proceeds. Since their truck was a small, lightly-built Italian vehicle, the first part of the plan was only a partial success; the impact knocked the gates partly open, but then the vehicle got stuck halfway through with its radiator shattered and spraying steam. Two of the bandits were in the cab and were effectively trapped there, but two more who had been in the truck bed jumped over the top and down into the yard. One of them, who had an AK, triggered off a burst at the back door of the depot.

Mike's security had, of course, been prepared for something very much like this. All three of the 'inventory' personnel were in position to cover the yard, and the one with the best view of the stalled truck happened to be the one with an M-60 machine gun. He put a long burst of fire directly into the cab, killing both of the raiders there and, as the rounds went through the back of the cab, fatally wounding another one who was still crouching behind. The other two Americans opened up with M-16s, finishing off the desperadoes who had actually gotten into the yard. The others, however many of them there were, fled in abject panic down the alley and off into the winding streets.

Mike didn't see any of this; he heard it, but it was over before he could unholster his pistol and get to the back. When he got there, he saw his people in position, reloading, looking for further threats, doing what shooters do when the shooting's stopped but might start up again. The next thing he saw, lying by the back door, was Liam the accountant, lying very still indeed.

Mike was not a lightning-fast thinker, and his immediate reactions, over the next hour, were all related to damage control. Liam was dead, killed by a round that had come right through the heavy wooden door. Five locals were dead, killed by weapons that were technically not supposed to be there. Attention had been drawn to the depot, something that was not supposed to happen at all. Officials who had been paid to make sure things like this did not take place had to be complained to, and they in turn had to complain back about negative publicity. The company had to be advised. The courier had to be headed off, since it might not be safe to try to get money out. The customer's new order had to be placed ...

Ah. And then Mike had a new thought. There was an amount of money in the safe that was on the books. There was a known and planned level of product to be delivered. And then there was the new order and the briefcase. Mike knew about it. Liam had known it was coming. Nobody else at Northern did.

After that, things moved along by themselves. Northern decided to shut down the Addis depot and set up something else in East Africa, using a new program manager. Mike was called home. He took the position that he'd been failed by the local officials, the company took the position that he'd failed to handle security. He offered his resignation. They accepted. When the customer eventually inquired about its two point seven million Euros' worth of goods, the company assumed they were being scammed by the customer, since they knew nothing about any such deal. People higher up in the customer organization assumed that people lower down had stolen the money, and they took measures, eliminating the only person other than Mike who knew about it. And eventually, after a complicated journey, the money ended up with the newly-retired Mike Calley.

The Mother of Sphinx

She was the mother of Sphinx, the deadly destroyer ...

It was late in the day on Wednesday when Jenn called Doug Markowitz's cell phone. There had been an internal struggle, her insecurities on one side arguing for a talk with MacArthur first and her self-respect telling her that she was perfectly capable of talking with a Fed on her own. She compromised by calling Doug, but promised herself that she'd stick strictly to facts. That lasted until she'd run down the limited number of real facts available; then Doug started asking questions.

"That fleeing thing in Rome sounds like crap," he said. "A beige pickup got away from one cop. How the hell do they know it was even Hagland?"

"That's not really clear," Jenn said. "The officer claimed a positive ID on someone going into a bar on foot, no connection with the truck. Then he went looking for the truck and saw something like it blow a stop sign. He never saw it again. Hagland was somebody the officer knew from a previous traffic stop, he said."

"And the cop didn't go back to the bar, either. Did Hagland make any kind of statement about it?"

"According to the record, he said he was never in Rome at all that night. But nothing to prove it."

"But then he gets busted for a hand to hand pot deal in Sturgis ...?"

"Not really," said Jenn. "When I talked to the officer down there, he didn't claim that was it. He saw Hagland's truck parked wrong, he pulled over, and Hagland ran. He was standing at the window of another truck, but that one drove off and got away, no ID, no good descriptions. The officer told me he guessed it was a deal, since Hagland was dropping packages of weed, but 'guess' was the word he used. And they only charged him with less than an ounce. Not delivery quantities."

"So it could have been anything, really."

"Well ..."

"Yeah?" said Doug. "What are you thinking?"

"He ran. He drew the attention to himself. Maybe there was something more than just weed in that other pickup truck."

"Um," said Doug. "Yeah, I suppose so."

"And there's this, too. Down in Sturgis, he had a fake ID, 'Phil Wayne', but there's no mention of that in the Rome thing, and the officer there didn't say anything about it."

"What does that do for us?"

"Well ... " Jenn paused. Did it do anything at all? "Well, I guess it tells me that up in Rome, they know Bobby Hagland, maybe better than they're admitting. Down in Sturgis, they don't know him at all."

"'They' being ...?"

"The cops. And I think there's a sort of a difference between Rome and Sturgis, maybe in your mind ...?"

"Yes, there is. Quite a difference."

"So ... " Another pause. "I guess it just says we really do want to talk to Bobby."

Once she got off the phone with Doug, Jenn called Mac. The number was busy because Doug had hit his speed-dial button just a hair quicker. Instead, she called Chief Fredricks, got through to his voicemail, and left him a sterile synopsis of what had been done and was being done, without mentioning any theories or using any code words; 'Rome' and 'cocaine' were left unsaid. Then she fiddled unenthusiastically with some paperwork for fifteen minutes or so. She was about to try Mac again when he called her.

The wonderful thing about telecommunication is that a group of people can be located in different places and at different times, sitting alone at desks or looking out windows, and they can still engage in groupthink. By a process it would be hard to describe, Mac and Jenn and Doug and Andy Patel, too, once Doug remembered to brief him, were beginning to see something foggy, misty, and uncertain in shape emerge around the person of Bobby Hagland. No one was willing to say "Hagland shot Rodney" or "Hagland knows who shot Rodney" or "Hagland knows why Rodney was shot." No one said that the unusual and slightly off-hand treatment of Hagland by the Rome cops was anything more than rookie behavior in a shattered department. But they were thinking it. Their interest in finding Bobby grew significantly. They'd have to wait another three days for it, though. At the same moment they were thinking about him, Bobby was driving east on Interstate 40, heading toward Albuquerque and a mistake that would cost him his life.

The Dreaded Serpent

> *... the dreaded serpent*
> *Who guards the apples of solid gold ...*

Mike Calley's business plan as he explained it to Gene was, as he said, both simple and complex. Somewhere in the world there would be someone with a commodity or an object to sell. Somewhere else, there would be someone who wanted it. Mike's enterprise, which became formalized between himself and Gene as 'Business 2', would find those people and connect them. The main asset would be Mike's knowledge of ways and means, governments and shippers and laws, buyers and sellers, and of course, the technologies themselves.

The actual methods would vary widely. Sometimes it would be all knowledge and no actual handling. For a fee or a slight increase in the price, Business 2 could execute a drop ship. A buyer would say, "I need such and such." Mike would locate the product and tell the seller who wanted it, the seller would get paid through Calley and ship the goods directly. It was the least profitable model, but also the least risky. For a much larger percentage, a buyer, typically a government agency or a group that aspired to be a government could get full service: acquisition, quality assurance, delivery. And if need be, Mike was prepared to set up a depot arrangement, similar to the one in Addis. That was rare, but it was very profitable indeed, and it was the primary reason he needed the farm and its barn and its shelving.

To Gene, this was a revelation. It was also an echo of his father's harebrained scheme. After all, Clay's farmland real estate idea had called for little or nothing except knowledge, connecting a source with a consumer. Looked at one way, Gene could be called clever for seeing that general pattern. Looked at another, one might wonder about his buying into it a second time. The difference was that this time, the scheme was workable; Calley did, in fact, have knowledge that people would pay for. Just as important, it was obvious that Calley had money to invest in the business. Gradually, as they got things in place, the deals began to occur. It turned out, to Gene's mild surprise, that Mike did actually know armaments people all over the world, and in a few months, there started to be boxes on the shelves and pallets stacked on the floor.

The rules as Mike laid them out were direct and easy to understand, and they all had to do with risk management. Rule one was that Mike and Gene themselves would never operate outside the US. When you're dealing with officials and businessmen and agencies overseas, you frequently have to provide incentives for people to cooperate with you. In many places, it's just a basic cost of doing business. But here at home, doing that is illegal. Among other statutes, it violates the Foreign Corrupt Practices Act, and that's a federal law, with a great big set of agencies to enforce it. So if anybody handed a mid-level bureaucrat an envelope of cash somewhere in, say, Africa, it would not be Mike Calley or Gene DeVoos. It would be someone quite else. And that person would not be in possession of any document or any other evidence that suggested Business 2's approval of bribing anybody.

Rule two was that they would stay small, as far as any one deal was concerned. Mike was adamant that Business 2 would make them both lots of money, but there would be no chasing the giant, multi-million dollar customer. If they kept each transaction down to half a million or a hundred thousand, and did a lot of those deals, they'd be far safer than they would be with big ones. It would be hard work for ten or fifteen years, and then they could both retire for good.

Rule three was to keep the number of people who knew anything about Business 2 to a severe minimum. This time, he mentioned the lawyer in Virginia; beyond that person, there was only Gene and Mike.

"We don't bring anybody else in unless," here, he almost said "I" but caught himself in time to say, "*we* agree ahead of time."

Over the following years, that was how they ran things. Gene kept an eye on the store and the local boys and girls who were hired to run it, sell the coffee, check IDs; it got a reputation for being very clean about sales to minors. Most of his time, though, Gene spent doing the operational work for Business 2. He learned to use spreadsheet software to keep lists and he learned how to encrypt them. He became good at airline reservations and shipping company procedures. He weatherproofed the barn, and he stage-managed a re-roofing project for the old house such that the workmen never had time to look sideways, let alone notice what might or might not be going on elsewhere on the farm. He learned about Internet service providers and secure servers and staying out of the cloud. Even the interaction with a neighbor who grew corn on the south field, under lease, came across Gene's desk, or desks, rather, since he had one open, public office at the back of the store and shared another in one of the bedrooms in the house. That one was always locked, and its door, like all the doors in the house, was curiously robust.

Calley spent a lot of time away, traveling around the US, sometimes because he really did need to be in Atlanta or Minneapolis or Newark, sometimes just because someone else was coming through, and there could be a meeting at an airport. He was not a rogue salesman type; he never promised more than he realistically thought they could deliver, and he never intentionally left Gene holding the bag. In a large company, a sales exec can say anything, get a big commission, and jump ship before the chickens came home to roost, but

Business 2 was really nothing more to its customers than Mike Calley. His reputation was everything, especially since many deals were done on a handshake or whatever the cultural equivalent might be. Mike had good reason to exhibit integrity.

For a long time, the deals were almost all brokering and phone calls and email, with either source or destination or both being overseas. There was some handling of inventory, some work that took place within the US, but not a lot. If heavy physical loads had to be moved, it happened on someone else's trucks, or in short term rentals, picked up from and returned to agencies a good distance away from Sturgis and company headquarters. But as the first decade of the twenty-first century wound down, the internal deals became more frequent and the quantities smaller, and Business 2 began to feel the need for a truck of its own. So nemesis manifests itself.

Humans

... and then the race of humans ...

"The truck," as both Mike and Gene called it, had a background of rejection. If it had been human, its role in the chaos-to-be could have been attributed to a lack of love and direction in its early life. As an inanimate object, a product of one of the world's largest industrial enterprises, it of course had no such psyche to be damaged. It was just a member of the cast without any lines, holding a spear and staring out into the audience.

In fact, it was a late 2010 Chevrolet Express van, ordered in Virginia by an optimistic young man who intended to get rich by becoming a handyman. His business plan evaporated before he could even take delivery of his new truck, sticking the dealer with it. It was very much a commodity vehicle, plain white, with solid sides, two seats, and lots of cargo room. It might have sold faster, but the original buyer had ordered it with a big five-point-three liter V8, his idea being that it would not only be his work truck but also pull his bass boat (which he would buy as soon as he got rich).

It sat on the dealer's lot in Falls Church for several months, and then was swapped with another dealer, up in Maryland. There, after some dickering, a commercial laundry bought it for a substantial discount. It took them less than three months to discover that their fuel bills for it were becoming a major component of their expense profile on each delivery, and they traded it back in at a Chrysler dealer, getting a reasonable price for it in their purchase of another van, this time with a six.

And there it was, in that dealer's online inventory, when Mike Calley located it. He wanted an anonymous-looking truck, and this one with its big engine, seemed like a good bet for hauling heavy cargo and maybe even pulling a trailer, if necessary. Neither he nor Gene were really car guys, although Gene knew more about it than Mike.

There were still a few things that Mike had not yet shared with Gene, even after eight years of association. One example was Professional Energy Research Associates, Incorporated, a Delaware company whose board of directors was listed as M. Patrick Calley, plus Mike's DC-area lawyer, and no one else. The list of employees was what's called in computing 'an empty set'. In fact, PERA was nothing at all except a legal fiction that assisted in moving money around from one place to another and, when it seemed like a good idea, assuming ownership of capital assets. The lawyer made a phone call or two, drove up to Maryland to look at the van, and it became one of those assets.

It sat in the lawyer's condo parking lot for a week, its sides still proclaiming it to be a laundry van. Mike was due for one of his quick trips down to the DC area anyway, and he flew from Detroit to Dulles at the end of a Thursday. The next morning, the lawyer picked him up at his hotel, and they drove back to the condos for a morning-long discussion, covering a long punch list of financial and legal trivia. At the end of it, the lawyer gave Mike the keys to the van, a Maryland registration, and a proof-of-insurance card. Mike left about two o'clock, spent the night in a Cleveland suburb, and rolled back into the Sturgis farm lot the next day.

Mike gave Gene the task of getting the van's laundry signage painted over, returning it to a plain white. He ordered a pair of magnetic door signs with the PERA name and logo. This was a surprise to Gene, as was Mike's announcement that the van was owned by something called PERA, but that Gene's name would be the point of contact. Gene objected mildly to this last stipulation, since he'd never heard of PERA.

"Okay," said Mike, waving a pencil like a wand. "Poof. You're a board member."

After a decent interval, Gene parked the van in an isolated spot up in Colon, near a bar he'd taken to visiting with a sort-of girlfriend. He took the Maryland license plate off and disposed of it, then reported the plate stolen. Shortly after, the van had a Michigan plate and registration, along with insurance in the name of PERA, using Gene's apartment address as the "Midwest Office." None of these levels of indirection would keep a determined investigation from linking Michael Calley with the van, but unless something happened involving high speed pursuit, a wreck, fatalities, and an elementary school destroyed by an explosion of mortar shells, any official problem related to the van would be unlikely to produce more than a traffic ticket for whichever member of the PERA board was driving.

So far, the van had done little more than transport Mike and Gene on various errands, and its carrying capacity had not been tested. But then one of those small, domestic deals appeared. Down in Tucson, a gun shop found itself in financial difficulties. Before filing for bankruptcy, the owner did some asking around among the fraternity of sportsmen who'd been his customers, the topic being inventory liquidation. In particular, he had a large amount of 7.62 NATO ammunition, almost exactly equivalent to .308 Winchester, by either name a rifle cartridge popular with deer hunters, snipers, and fans of slightly out-of-date military small arms. If he could get cash out of this stock, he could stave off the most pressing of his creditors, buy enough time to pack certain things up, and move quietly out of state.

His asking around led him to Mike, and Mike ran a hard deal. The owner wanted the stuff gone, fast and in one parcel. Mike wanted the absolute best price he could get, since there was plenty of the .308 round available. There'd be no point in his getting involved unless he could offer one of his overseas customers a really good price on it. They did a bit of figuring on the phone, mostly about weight and size, and he concluded that it could all fit in the van and make it back to Michigan in one long round trip. They agreed and set a date.

Then Gene, the operations man, suggested they test the van first. He'd already talked Mike into letting him install a modified lock box, a small, rectangular container bolted under the chassis to hold cash and documents. Now, he proposed they take the truck into the barn, fire up the propane-powered forklift they were leasing, and see what happened when you loaded pallets of ammunition onto a laundry van.

The results were not encouraging. The handyman back in Virginia had ordered a big engine for towing, but he'd assumed that General Motors would take care of commercial-quality suspension. As a general case, this was true. GM's engineers had made reasonable assumptions about how much laundry or how many tools or how dense a wedding cake anyone might need to haul around in the 3500. But pallets of small arms ammunition were not among the things they allowed for; one test pallet caused the truck to sag, and if it was placed anywhere back of the central point, the front suspension unloaded noticeably. The shipment from Tucson would be four pallets in all, plus the weight of full fuel tanks and the driver. For a trip into town, you could live with it. For a run of almost four thousand miles, down to Arizona and back, something could very easily break.

That was about five o'clock in the afternoon. Gene went back into the store to check on the pair of local kids who were running things and to get on the Internet and see about suspension kits. Mike, annoyed and distracted, slid under the van to see the lockbox; he hadn't had time to look at it.

Because there was nothing in it, it wasn't locked. The box itself had been repurposed from a pistol safe; it was flat, about two inches thick, and had a three-finger lock mechanism. In its new location, the lock was on top where it could be felt but not seen. Like many of Mike's security arrangements, it was not designed to defeat a detailed effort, just to blend in.

Outside, the day's off-and-on rain started up again, sounding worse on the barn roof than it actually was. In Mike's left back pocket, a bulky shape pressed against his hip, reminding him that he'd forgotten one thing while he was passing through airports. He had seventeen hundred Euros in cash, rolled up and rubber-banded; a gentleman in a Chicago suburb, but originally from Boyle, in the County Roscommon (as he always introduced himself), had given it to him in return for a specific piece of hardware, technically illegal in America and extremely illegal in Ireland. This fellow was not much of a customer, but Mike kept on doing small bits of business with him on the theory that he might be connected to something larger. He'd meant to exchange the Euros for dollars at either Detroit or Dulles, but it had slipped his mind.

The barn's human-sized door opened, and Gene walked around to the side of the van where Mike's feet were sticking out. "Six hundred dollars or so," he said. "Helper springs in the back and probably a sway bar, too. Plus labor."

Mike put the Euros into the lock box, to see if it would still close and latch. It did. "How much did you say?" he asked, crawling out from under the truck.

"Six hundred. There's all kinds of after-market stuff out there."

"Can we get it overnighted?" Mike crawled back out, leaving the money in the still-unlocked box.

"Sure," said Gene, "But we need somebody else to put it on. I wouldn't want to trust my work on something like that, with all that weight in there."

"Well, hell," said Mike. "Who can we get? I don't want just anybody fussing with it. Even that sign shop guy was too curious for my taste."

"I need to change clothes ... I'm meeting Lynn up in Colon. Maybe there'll be somebody up there. You want me to just get it done, if I can get it done quietly?"

"Yeah. Freeway speeds, light on the front wheels, some idiot ahead jumps on the brakes. I don't want to think about it."

"Van crash spills ammunition on freeway. Homeland Security claims terrorist plot."

"Right," said Mike. "That's what I don't want. Exactly that." He had already forgotten leaving the money in the box. It was, after all, at least two and even three orders of magnitude less than his usual deals involved, and the customer's constant political chatter had given Mike the notion that he was just a political crank; as things turned out, he was quite wrong about that.

"Okay," said Gene. "I'll go order the parts now and see if I can get somebody to put 'em on, like, day after tomorrow." It was the evening of March 22nd. The following day, Rodney Garfield would be released from jail. He had eighteen days to live.

A Most Terrible Child

... she bore a most terrible child ...

Back in his cell at Macomb Correctional, Big Willy McDivitt was feeling better. He didn't always like to admit it, but that little brother of his was damn smart. "When you runnin' from the police," the kid had said, "you take your cigarettes and throw 'em in the street. You throw a lighter down the other way. Easy to see, easy to find. Then you get rid of your stash someplace smart where it ain't easy to find. You let 'em find the smokes and the lighter, but they don't find the stuff."

"So?"

"So that's what we gotta do. We gotta throw somethin' down."

Smart kid, no denying it. Big Willy felt a lot better.

Against Those Winds

... no defense
Against those winds when men meet them at sea.

The bar in Colon where Gene and his friend were going to meet was divided into drinking and talking space, and dining space. The dining part was better lit and more family-focused than the bar itself. They ate, and Gene had the one beer he usually drank in an evening. Lynn had a soda, since she was leaving after dinner for her shift at an urgent-care center. After she'd gone, Gene would normally have headed back to his apartment in Sturgis, but tonight there was still the task of locating a capable and preferably informal mechanic. He settled the dinner tab, then moved to the bar side, ordered one more beer, and sounded out the bartender about car repair. This produced nothing beyond an obvious suggestion to try a Chevy dealer.

"I could," Gene objected, "but I got the parts already ordered. A dealer's not going to want to install my parts. And their labor's expensive."

"Maybe so," said the bartender. "I don't really know anybody. I always take my car to the dealer." A customer at the far end of the bar waved an empty glass, and the bartender moved away to fill it.

"'Scuse me," said a young man one bar stool away. "I work on cars and stuff."

Bobby Hagland was far short of his four-beer limit. He'd only gotten to Colon a short while before, and he was husbanding his money, anyway. He moved over next to Gene, and explored the nature of the work that needed to be done. He was used to exaggerating his skills and expertise, and this seemed like something he could do easily. Indiana Jim was a no-show, so far, and a little income right now would be a good thing. He and Gene finished what they were drinking, and they walked outside to examine the truck, sitting where Gene had parked it.

Hagland talked up his background in repair, inventing a dealership job from which he said he was temporarily laid off, due to the damn economy. Gene said sympathetic things about hard times, and offered what he thought was a low-balled amount, expecting Bobby to come back with a counter offer. Instead, he accepted it. Gene hid his surprise, and they shook hands on it.

"Can you do it on Saturday?" he asked. "We're down south of here, outside Sturgis."

Sturgis was not the city name Bobby would have preferred to hear, and this being Thursday night, it left him with an entire day to kill, probably in the area, since he didn't want to spend the gas to go back and forth from Milan again before getting paid. But despite his limitations, he was moderately resourceful when he was given this kind of simple tactical problem. He dealt with the Sturgis issue by giving Gene the name on his now-confiscated fake ID, Phil Wayne, and got instructions to the farm, promising to be out there around nine AM. The killing time problem, especially the problem of where to spend at least two nights for little or no money, he'd solved before.

Even in an increasingly monitored and secure America, there are places where parking your vehicle and sleeping in it are not crimes nor are they suspicious acts. Many of the exits from the interstate highway system offer truck stops where long haul drivers pull off, crawl into semi-tractor cabins, campers, or just the back seat, and catch up on their sleep. Bobby had used a couple of them over this way already, and they were a much safer bet than parking on a rural roadside or a city street. He spent Thursday night at one place, visited a couple of small towns aimlessly on Friday, picked another freeway exit for that evening, and on Saturday morning, pulled into the parking lot of Calley's store. The girl at the counter pointed him at Gene's office, and the two men headed out back to the barn.

Gene had used part of Friday to do some background checking on Hagland. Since he was checking on Phil Wayne, though, he got little useful information. The Phil Waynes he found didn't match very well with the young man he was employing, but he'd followed Mike Calley's basic instructions: "Run a check on anybody we hire." For the store, this was easy. High school kids out here in the countryside didn't have a lot of time to pile up criminal records or to join terrorist groups. If their behavior was on the questionable side, there was often a certain amount of pressure applied to keep it out of the public eye. For a part-time, self-employed mechanic, it was something else again. On one hand, Gene didn't find any evidence that anyone named Phil Wayne had done anything that would rule him out as someone to install aftermarket parts on a van. Turn it around and you get the question: is this really Phil Wayne at all? But the deal was done, Wayne was here, the parts were here, and Gene could tell Mike he'd done the checking.

In the barn, the goods on the shelves were draped with tarpaulins. The shapes were mostly rectangular solids and could have been anything. Nothing visible, if you looked around, would suggest anything at all about the nature of the 'wholesale supply' business Gene had mentioned. He even remembered that Bobby would probably notice the lockbox under the van, but since Gene believed it was empty, he was not concerned. And because Bobby was mostly interested in getting the job done quickly and getting paid, he didn't see the box right away.

When he finally did, lying under the blocked-up truck and checking his work on the bolts, he was initially puzzled. The van was a newer vehicle than he'd worked on before, but still, this didn't look like original equipment. He slid his hands around it, found the lock and opening mechanism, and watched as the lid dropped. What it spilled onto his chest was a roll of money, not a kind he'd seen before, but obviously money.

Ethics was not a frequent topic of self-examination for Bobby. As far as he knew, he'd finish up this job in the next ten or so minutes, get three hundred dollars from Gene, and never see him again. He'd have to stay out of Colon, but that was a minor issue. And they didn't have his real name. He was just smart enough to resist taking the whole amount, though. Instead, he removed seven hundred Euros from the center of the roll, put it in his front jeans pocket, held the rest back in the box and closed it up again.

While Bobby was beefing up the van, Gene and Mike were confronting a schedule problem. Mike had been called by an old acquaintance, a very senior non-commissioned officer in the armed forces of El Salvador, a gentleman with wide access to equipment of the kind Mike needed for a buyer in another hemisphere. This NCO, Staff Sergeant Alejandro Obregón, was fond of the United States and enjoyed traveling north of the various borders; he was proposing – strongly proposing – a visit to Calley's farm to talk business, and that visit would overlap with the pickup in Arizona. That let Calley out of consideration to make the trip.

For his part, Gene could go, but the store and many other aspects of the business would be left in Mike's hands, then, for at least four days. During those four days, there were tasks to be accomplished that Sergeant Obregón should not really witness, and Mike would have no way to park him or, frankly, keep him out of trouble while standing in for Gene.

And of course, checking with the bankrupt shop owner in Arizona got them no slack. He'd already cut his price for the .308 ammunition to the bone. Neither party could afford to pay for shipping it, nor did they want the records that would create. The owner was adamant: he needed somebody down there with a truck on April eleventh, period. And Mike had discovered that, counter to expectations, he really did need this purchase to make good on a larger, more important order.

Gene, for his part, was beginning to develop a minor attitude about his role in Business 2. He was the second in command, the one who kept the lights on and the wheels greased, and he didn't care for the idea of a four thousand mile drive in a truck filled with ammunition of dubious legality. Travel was all right, but he liked flying to destinations with beaches and young women, not driving through deserts populated with dusty old men. And so he bent the truth a bit.

"You know, Mike," he said. "I did some background work on this guy who's fixing up the van. He came up clean, no problems. We could get him to go."

To say that this proposal met with resistance is to understate the case. Mike was not convinced by Internet background checks. He was concerned enough just about having someone in the barn who hadn't been "cleared," let alone sending someone like that on a product run. No, he couldn't define "cleared," precisely, except that it meant someone who a) he trusted and b) had something big to lose.

Gene had counter arguments. Bobby did have something to lose: he was unemployed, needed a job, needed income. He, Gene, had tracked Bobby down, not vice versa (another lie; he hadn't described to Mike the contact in the Colon bar, but it certainly didn't amount to his having "tracked down" anybody). And most telling, they needed the Arizona product, and they couldn't have Obregón running around loose in Western Michigan, drinking American cocktails and chasing Western Michigan co-eds. Of the few associates who came in person, most were low-key, covert, and flying under the radar. Obregón was none of those things. And they needed a deal with him. Long before Gene convinced Mike, Gene had convinced himself. Bobby was his find, and now he was invested in him.

So the outcome was that when Gene went back to the barn, he had the grudging approval of Calley to offer Bobby another job: that of driving the van down to Arizona, picking up four pallets of 'goods', and coming back with them. Bobby had a bad moment, thinking about the seven hundred Euros, but he didn't turn the offer down. The pay was more than he usually made in months, and the trip was a new thing; he'd never been south of the Ohio River. And it was far enough off in time that he could go home, clean up, and hide the strange money he had in his pocket. In fact, he didn't need to be back in Sturgis until the eighth.

"Come down here in the evening," Gene told him, "And you can stay at the house, get briefed on the trip, and head out the next day. Monday, April ninth."

The Ashwood Mortals

To the ashwood mortals who live on the earth.

Staff Sergeant Alejandro Obregón was a member of *Ejército Salvadoreño*, the Army of El Salvador. He was assigned to the First Brigade, and he'd spent some time in Iraq with the Coalition. He was crooked as a split rail fence, having a toe in the world of Salvadoran gangs and another in the semi-official death squads that hypothetically existed to hunt the gangs down. He augmented his pay by any number of private means, and for Calley, he was an important source of certain kinds of small arms parts that would otherwise be hard to come by. He was also a loose cannon.

He flew into Baltimore from El Salvador International, took a cab to Dulles and then a connection to Detroit; Calley met him at the terminal. Obregón was wearing civilian clothing with a curiously military cut. If the man owned anything that wasn't olive drab or camouflage, Calley had never seen it. His rolled up shirtsleeves also showed a large bandage on his left forearm. Mike carefully shook the right hand and inquired about the wound.

"Snake," said Obregón. "Bastard was in tree, I don't see him."

Where Mike had grown up, there were no venomous snakes, and in all of Michigan, there was only one small, ineffective rattlesnake species. The notion of getting bitten just by walking past a tree was appalling.

"Not bad, I hope?" he said.

"No. I get small, what is the word? ... poison from him. Not much, you see?"

"What kind of snake was it?"

"*Gammarrilla*, maybe. Don't know. I blow him to fucking hell with shotgun."

All Mike could think of to say about that was "Ah." He knew enough about Obregón that his having been out in the snake-infested bush, hunting with a shotgun, was not surprising.

What he was hunting was not something Mike wanted to know. Consequently, the conversation remained social and trivial as they walked out to the SUV. Leaving the airport, Mike carried out some rudimentary moves to ensure that they weren't being followed, then headed back toward the farm. On the drive they talked business. Finally, Obregón brought up what Calley knew he would, recreation and equipment. The Sergeant patted his right hip.

"Nothing there," he said. "I don't feel good with no *pistola*. You can loan me this?"

"Sure," said Mike. "How about a forty-five?" Arming a man like Obregón was a minor security problem, but by now there were more untraceable guns in Mike's possession than legal ones, and letting Obregón carry one around under his shirt was actually the least risky aspect of this whole relationship. The man was a long-serving soldier, after all. He wouldn't shoot anybody without good reason.

"A Colt? Yes, good. Better than mine."

"Fine. Remind me when we get to the farm. I'll dig out a holster, too."

"Good, good, my old friend. And maybe some fun, too? There are women in this town, Sturgees?"

"Ah, well now, Sergeant, we have to be careful what we do around the farm. We'll go somewhere nearby, maybe. Chicago would be good."

"Chicago! Yes! It is close?"

"Close enough," said Mike. *And far enough away, too, you crazy son of a bitch.*

Droves of Cattle

> *Droves of cattle, herds of goats on a plain …*

The store and the rest of the Calley operation sat on the north side of county Highway 215. The farm was near the road's western end, where it ran into Highway 66. Past the farm, it led due east, straight as a die, for four and a half miles more. It crossed several north/south roads, and it finally turned into an unpaved dead-end in a stand of woods. Along the way, two houses sat across from each other, the one on the north associated with a working farm, the one on the south, a new house on a two-acre lot that a farmer had subdivided and sold to his son. The farmer was dead now and the son had moved away, selling the little house to a husband and wife who were not by birth country people. Mr. Fisher worked in an insurance agency in Sturgis, and Mrs. Fisher kept house and harbored small dogs.

Across the road, the fields were still being worked by a farming family, but the old house was a rental property, and the renters, the Coburns, kept a trio of goats. On the afternoon of the Eleventh, Sturgis officer Tracy Douglas, responding to an out-county call, drove up 66 to 215 and east to the Fisher house. This was his third trip there in a month, since it seemed that Mrs. Coburn's goats were again loose and again chasing Mrs. Fisher's schnauzers. He dealt with it diplomatically, encouraging the ladies to stop berating each other, and the goats to return to their own side of the highway. On the way back, he stopped at Calley's store for a cup of coffee. He said hello to Gene DeVoos and to the boy behind the counter, paid for his coffee, and drove off. Douglas was the same officer who had arrested Bobby Hagland and who had spoken with Jenn; at this point, he still owed her a call back, although it would only be to say that he couldn't locate that false ID Bobby had used.

Next morning, Thursday the twelfth, Douglas started his shift and was immediately assigned a repeat visit to the Fisher/Coburn households. In the early hours, the goats, masters of the art of escape, had again gotten out and done some form of damage to the Fisher yard or perhaps porch; the complaint wasn't especially clear on the details. A goat had also chased a dog or dogs and "threatened" Mr. Fisher as he left for work. Officer Douglas had many years on the job, and he was resigned to this sort of thing. He handled it well, resorting to the old "What are we going to have to do to resolve this?" approach, and getting Mrs. Coburn to admit that her fencing was not really up to par. It took up a good thirty minutes of the taxpayers' time, but when he was finally able to clear from the call, he felt he'd earned his morning coffee and maybe even a doughnut, and he headed back west toward Calley's store.

When he pulled in to the small parking lot, his car was one of three. A woman walked out of the store with a small bag and got into a blue Saturn that was nearest the door. Back at the end of the lot, where Douglas assumed employees would be told to park, was a beige-gold Chevrolet S-10 pickup, and it occurred to him that he'd seen it there before, yesterday in fact.

Worth a look, he thought and strolled over to where he could see the plate. But when he reached for his notebook, he realized he didn't have it. It was somewhere in his bedroom at home, most likely on the dresser or still in the pocket of yesterday's uniform shirt. The notebook would have told him whether or not this truck was the one Bobby Hagland was driving; as it was, all he could do was find something else to write on and record the plate. And of course, he could ask in the store about whose truck it was.

Inside, the clerk was a different person from yesterday, a boy whose name tag said 'Jerry'. Douglas poured a large coffee, selected a pastry, and asked about the S-10. Jerry said he didn't really know, it was a guy who did some work for Mr. DeVoos. The truck had been there this morning when he, Jerry, came in, but he didn't know any more than that. And no, Mr. DeVoos wasn't around.

Well, well. Back outside, Douglas put his purchases in the police car and walked back to the Chevy. It was locked, and the Plexiglas windows on the cab were too weathered to permit much of an examination of the bed. Inside the cab he could see debris of various kinds, fast food wrappers and so on. Nothing obviously incriminating and nothing to connect it with the guy that Ann Arbor detective was looking for. But it was the right kind of truck, and it was here in the Sturgis area. When he got back in town, he'd either swing by his house for the notebook or drop in at the station to call Langton. He had a personal cell phone, but its calls were on his nickel, and already, even in his forties, he was thinking frugally, looking forward to retiring and forgetting all about Mrs. Coburn and her damn goats.

The clerk, Jerry Bien, was one of Gene's crew. Usually, Gene got recommendations through the high school counselors, looking to place students who needed starter jobs or resume building, but Jerry was an exception. He'd been home-schooled by his father after the mother passed away. Bien Senior was a grim, unhappy man, living on a mortgaged forty-acre farm and working another two hundred acres on lease. Nothing worked out very well for him, it seemed. If anybody was going to have equipment problems in the middle of harvest, it would be him. If a tax return was going to be audited, it would be his. Only the boy was any kind of a success, at least from the father's perspective. He was a healthy kid, his teeth didn't need straightening, he didn't develop a desire to be a pianist or a ballet dancer, and he could drive a tractor in a straight line. He was respectful and attentive, and he didn't object when he found himself pulled out of school over a dispute about curriculum. The old man had been brought up in a fundamentalist creed, and the schools he attended never touched on anything very philosophical, at least as he remembered it. It came as a shock to discover that the kids in Jerry's classes weren't saying the Pledge of Allegiance and were being fed that wicked evolution stuff as though it were gospel.

As a consequence, Jerry got the last two years of his education from the Bible, a few old standard text books, and his old man's embittered world view. He didn't come out of it as an accomplished mathematician or a progressive social theorist, but he did get a grounding in edgy right-wing thought, including the desirability of small government and the absolute necessity of guarding yourself and your family against an apocalyptic event of some kind. Like most of the boys he knew, he was a hunter and a relatively good shot; unlike most of them, he had a fixed notion that sooner or later, he and Dad and maybe some other folks would need to use their guns in defense of their liberties. It wasn't a burning passion or something that kept him up at night; it was more of an article of faith. He was a Good American, and periodically, Good Americans had to stand up and assert their rights.

He saw a 'Help Wanted' note at the store, applied, and got hired. It came as no surprise at all to Jerry when part of the training Gene gave him included the Mossberg twelve gauge shotgun that was always kept behind the store's counter. The doctrine was very simple; it never was to come out or get shown to anybody unless that person was armed and trying to commit a crime in the store. It never was to be fired unless it was clear that not firing it would result in staff or a customer being injured or killed. In fact, all of this came down from Calley who intended it for Gene, but Gene passed it on to the boys and girls he hired. Among his reasons for doing that was the fact that it helped him distance himself from the unglamorous store and its mundane aspects. It also helped ensure that if anyone actually shot a robber, it wouldn't be Gene who did the shooting. He had his own methods of managing risk.

The Sheer Deception

The sheer deception, irresistible to men ...

Around three o'clock on Sunday the eighth, Bobby parked the S-10 at the rear of the store parking lot. Apparently, nobody had noticed the dip he'd taken into the lockbox cash; nothing was said about it, anyway. It didn't occur to him to ask about leaving the truck parked out front, and it didn't occur to Gene, who was a busy man that afternoon, to ask where he'd left it. Instead, both of them focused on getting the details of the trip squared away.

Gene had a couple of maps for Bobby, one on a very small scale, showing a freeway route from Michigan to Arizona, with a stay in Oklahoma City on Monday night, then on to Tucson on Tuesday. The larger scale map showed where the gun store was and specified Wednesday morning as the time to show up. He had Bobby coming back a slightly different way, leaving time for loading up and only getting as far as Albuquerque before stopping over. Gene also provided cash for meals and hotels, calculated to leave Bobby a tip if he selected reasonably-priced lodging. For gas and emergencies, there was a company debit card, and he gave Bobby a cheap cell phone to call in.

"It's going to be a long few days driving," he said. "Don't get too burned out. As long as you make the date on the eleventh, the details don't matter too much, but I think this route and these stops are your best bet. And stay in touch. Call me when you make stops and especially when you have the goods on board."

"Got it," said Bobby. "Do I pay this guy for the stuff I'm picking up?"

"No. That's handled already. We'll pay him once you call and tell us you're on your way back, with the products."

"And do I get to know what the stuff is?"

"It's just industrial bits and pieces. I'm not entirely sure what all it is, myself," Gene said. "Mr. Calley deals with that end of things. I just make the pickups and deliveries happen." This was, of course, an egregious lie, but Gene was feeling a bit paranoid, now that the trip was kicking off, and he wanted Bobby in the dark as much as possible. He'd asked the seller to wrap the pallets in something opaque, as a gesture to security.

"Okay," said Bobby. "I don't really care, anyway." This was also a lie, since the work he'd done on the truck, the presence of the lockbox, and the Euros he'd pocketed all pointed to a cargo of something interesting, heavy, and in quantity.

Gene showed Bobby a room in the upstairs of the farmhouse, one of two kept as bedrooms for visitors. Sergeant Obregón had the other, but he and Calley were elsewhere. *Just as well*, Gene thought. *I don't really want to do any introductions with that wild-ass guy or have him ask any of his questions*; sometimes, Obregón could be remarkably direct, especially with people he saw as subordinates. There was a small TV set in the room, hooked to a dish, and he suggested that Bobby relax for an hour or so and then they'd go get some dinner. That was fine with Bobby. Uncharacteristically, he got to bed at a relatively early hour.

He was already awake when Gene knocked on his door, Monday morning. They'd both managed to miss Calley and Obregón coming home from somewhere, Mike tense and sober, Obregón jolly, expansive, singing something bawdy in Spanish. Bobby heard it, but he kept his light out and his door shut, not wanting any more contact than necessary with the man who was obviously the boss of this whole show, and none at all with whoever the drunk he had with him might turn out to be. He just wanted to get on the road, get the job done, and fade away with his proceeds.

To get where he had to go, the most direct drive was also a nasty drive, at least in its early stages. It started with a high-traffic, highly-used loop around the southeast corner of the Chicago sprawl, until you could get on I-57. Then it was a long

144

haul south through Illinois to I-70, picking up I-44 in St Louis, and heading out west. By the time Bobby got to cross the Mississippi, he was already sick of the plains states. The sight of the Arch from the Poplar Street bridge didn't make up for the tedium, especially since he didn't know what it was. The tangle of highways kept his attention on exits and directions, and he was well out of town before the slight improvement in scenery made an impression. He passed his second Springfield of the trip, angled down southwest past Loma Linda and just south of the Kansas line, and headed into Oklahoma. Finally, after a longer day on the road than he'd spent in his life, he found a Comfort Inn just off the freeway, in an Oklahoma City suburb.

Next morning, he bought gas and beef jerky and pointed the van west again. He ran across the Texas Panhandle, past Amarillo and on into New Mexico, unaware that part of the way followed the famous old US Route 66 (motto: 'Yes, *that* Route 66'.) The scenery was more entertaining now; Tucumcari gave him a view of an actual mesa, for example, and as he approached Albuquerque, Sandia Peak began to loom up out of the horizon. If he'd ever heard of it, *House Carpenter* and its reference to the hills of hell looming dark and low might have come to mind. Since Bobby wasn't a folk music enthusiast, the moment of prescience was lost.

After a burger in Albuquerque, he drove on, this time south on I-25, taking the last leg down and west to Tucson and missing, though he didn't know it, the notorious checkpoint trap at Sierra Blanca, a half-horse town in Texas that specialized in busting musicians' tour buses as they came and went from Austin. The place names became more and more Hispanic, the landscape wilder and dryer. Finally, westbound on I-10, the dry washes and angry, empty desert outside Benson brought to the front of Bobby's mind the thought, *I'm a long damn way from home*. At long last: Tucson; he rolled past Davis-Monthan Air

Force Base, past Sentinel Peak, and into a Holiday Inn off St. Mary's.

Bobby was a tired boy on Wednesday morning, but he managed to get out of bed and suck down enough of the free buffet coffee to get himself kick-started. He found the gun shop without much trouble. It was a small building, set back from a four-lane street, with a 'Closed' sign on the door. Before he could knock, a man who looked as though he'd spent his life in the sun, ruddy red in the face and dried-out in general, opened up for him.

"You here from Mike Calley?" he asked.

"Yeah," said Bobby. "What are we loading up?"

"The pallets are in back," said the owner. "Pull your truck around, and we'll load it." Bobby noted that although he'd asked "What?" the man had answered "Where." Not a surprise.

As each of the four pallets settled into the back of the van, Bobby looked at the suspension, somewhat gratified that it didn't sag much more than he'd thought it would. The aftermarket equipment Gene bought was worth the money, apparently. Loading with a baby forklift took just twenty minutes, and Bobby signed for the load on what seemed to be an ad hoc form, run off on a laser printer. The man didn't offer him a copy.

"Long way to come for just that amount of ... stuff," he said and got a completely non-committal reply. Each pallet was wrapped in black plastic and for all he could tell, it might as well have been canned tuna. But he had another thirty-six or more hours, with an overnight stop, in which to snoop. Right now, all there remained to do in Tucson was gas up and head out.

Gene's suggested routes reflected some thought on his part. Instead of just sending Bobby back the way he'd come, he'd allowed for loading time, and so he sent him on a shorter route for the rest of Wednesday, one that would still get him out of Arizona but not be too long a drive, not for the first day's worth of fully-loaded driving. So instead of taking I-10 back east, Bobby drove northwest toward Phoenix, with Wasson Peak hovering on the left and, a bit later, Dove Mountain on the right. It's a quick hundred miles, give or take, from Tucson to Phoenix, and there wasn't a lot to see, but after Bobby picked up I-17 due north out of town, the look of the land got a lot more interesting. 17 is the Black Canyon Freeway, and it doesn't take long before the development tapers off, the north and southbound lanes separate and rejoin as they weave around the topography, and there are honest-to-God cartoon-style cactuses growing. It was the least Michigan-like country Bobby had ever seen, and after he got over his fuel-gauge paranoia (the heavily-loaded van was sucking gas like mad), he actually began to enjoy himself. Somewhere north of Black Canyon City, as the road skirted along the slopes of a mesa, he had the thought that if his issues with a driver's license — that is, not having one — could be resolved, maybe being a truck driver wouldn't be such a bad thing. Later, a sign for 'Horsethief Basin Recreational Area' made him wonder if maybe he shouldn't move out here. It seemed like his kind of place. He abandoned the rock and roll station that was on the radio and found a country channel instead.

On and on he went, in a classic American freeway flight, half-noticing as the flora changed from sage and cactus to pine trees; Bobby rolled past Mountainaire and on to Flagstaff, I-40 east, and a gas stop. He called Gene, as he'd been doing all along when he stopped, then got some take-out lunch and hit the road again. Five hours to go, half way across Arizona and half way across New Mexico to Albuquerque.

Winslow, Houck, across the state line into New Mexico, Gallup, over the continental divide, down into Grants, and finally, seen from the west this time, Sandia Peak and Albuquerque again. For a so-called short day, it seemed damn long to Bobby, long and thirsty. He passed up the first motel he saw on the grounds that there wasn't a bar, but the next place had one, and he checked in.

To this point in the trip, Bobby had been playing by the rules, at least as he understood them. He'd stayed on script with the route and the schedule, called in faithfully, and left the pallets alone. He'd been a careful and legal driver, although mostly out of self-interest. He'd kept his usual driving attitude under wraps, despite many provocations from other drivers on all those long miles. Now he was tired and the novelty of the whole thing was wearing off. Tonight, he wanted two things, no, three things. He wanted to know what was in the van's load, he wanted a good long sleep, and he wanted a beer or two. That was an unordered list, and he decided to start with the beers.

He chose a stool at the motel's bar and ordered a burger and a draught. There was a basketball game of some kind on the television, and he allowed most of his brain function to idle down, concentrating on the large, unwieldy hamburger and his beer, paying little or no attention to anything else. Consequently, the man who sat down next to him had to ask twice, "You Roger?"

"Huh?" Bobby managed after getting a bite of his dinner out of the way. "Roger?"

"Yeah," said the man, a slight, Hispanic-looking person, with a small mustache. "Are you Roger?"

"Nope," said Bobby. "Don't know any Roger."

"Damn, I thought you were. He's late. Supposed to meet him here, but he didn't show."

"Sorry, don't know him." Bobby paused, assuming that the man would now go away. After a pause, he added, "I'm passing through ... just stayin' here tonight."

"Okay, bro, no problem." A long pause ... "You, uh, you wouldn't want some smoke, would you?"

"Smoke?"

"Yeah, I got some for this Roger guy. Don't want to waste the drive over here, you know?"

"Maybe. Any good?" Bobby's interest rose sharply. With his pay for the suspension job and the leftover from Gene's hotel money (and Gene had been generous with it) he might be able to afford a small amount of weed. His inventory had been depleted by the Sturgis fiasco, and he assumed that he'd go back to his usual low-level dealing when he got this truck-driving gig over with.

"Oh, yeah, real good. From down in Chiapas, just over the fence yesterday." That meant nothing to Bobby, but it sounded impressive.

"Okay, how ... " he paused as the bartender came into earshot and took the other man's order for a Corona. "How much?"

Although he was almost intuitively familiar with the economics of marijuana in the upper Midwest, Bobby knew nothing about the sometimes linear, sometimes logarithmic increases in price as the product travelled away from its sources. He'd been thinking of an ounce or two but here in Albuquerque, it turned out that he could get almost twice that amount for the money he could spend. The potential profit, plus the cachet of being able to say, "Yeah, I got it down in New Mexico," to his Michigan customers sealed the deal.

The two finished their drinks and one at a time paid up and strolled off to the men's room. The transfer took place under adjacent stall partitions, and when Bobby had shoved the baggies into various pockets and opened his door, the man was already gone. His first inclination was to go up to his room and stash the weed in his duffle bag, but then he thought of the van, the lockbox, and those intriguing pallets. *Somebody installed that box for a reason*, he thought, *and this is as good a reason as any*.

One problem that he faced almost daily was his lack of ID. As has been noted already, he was not by any means the sharpest crayon in the box, but he did have a substantial amount of exposure to police procedures and to the average officer's general skepticism about motives and intentions. To put it simply, if a cop drove through the parking lot while Bobby was crawling around under the van, he would want to know why and, much worse, he'd want to know who Bobby was. Right now, he didn't have any identification with him at all, false or real, let alone a driver's license from any state in the union; that would lead to very unfortunate outcomes. On top of that, if his parole officer had managed to get her head above water long enough to check up on him, he'd have that set of problems under his real name. And finally, it wouldn't take a random cop driving by to cause trouble; motels had security cameras for their parking lots, plus any number of snoopy people. Someone might actually call 911 if they saw him doing something unusual.

So when he stepped out the back door of the place, he was nervous. He saw quickly, though, that fortune seemed to have favored him. He'd backed into a space at the rear of the lot, and a blank wall sheltered the back of the van. There was a large Ford SUV on the truck's left side, and someone had parked a horse trailer on the right; together, they blinded all but the front of the Express. If he went under the van from the left side, nobody but possibly the owner of the trailer would be able to see it, and then only if he happened to pay it a visit.

It took only a few minutes; he dropped to one knee at the left front of the van as though checking something about the tire, then flipped onto his back and wriggled underneath. The strange money (which a misunderstood conversation with a friend back in Milan had led him to think of as 'French') was still there. He stuffed his weed around it, made sure the box was securely latched, and crawled back out. He stood up in the cover of the trailer, brushed himself off, and walked around to the driver's door. He ostentatiously unlocked it with the key, establishing his ownership to anyone who might be watching, and got in. The load took up all the cargo space; there was no way to move around in the back. Any examination he did would have to be done on the front-most pallet, and on the front side of that.

The product, whatever it was, had been wrapped in black plastic, using a turntable-like device that spun each pallet vertically while winding the shrink-wrap around it. Normally, this would leave the top exposed, but someone had carefully covered each one with cardboard, prior to the wrapping. Bobby poked around for a bit, found a place at the bottom where the wrap hadn't been carefully taken around the pallet itself, and pulled as much away as he dared. To his frustration, all he could see was more black plastic. After some more feeling and prodding, he concluded that the load, whatever it was, was in small rectangular boxes, inside heavy plastic sleeves. The sleeve he could actually see was turned such that its markings were almost completely obscured; all he could read was part of a word in some non-English language and the number 7.6-something. It was annoying, but he was also played out and short at least one more beer. He gave up, locked the van, and went back inside to the bar.

Luck acts in strange ways. An hour later, an Albuquerque cop did drive through the lot, saw nothing unusual, didn't even see the van, and kept on going. If she'd been early enough to spot

Bobby crawling out from under the Chevy, she'd have saved at least four lives.

The next day's trip back is scarcely worth describing. Bobby stuck to the script as far as south-central Illinois when, out of sheer boredom, he checked his map and took I-70 east into Indiana, around Indianapolis, and then north on I-69 all the way back into Michigan, hitting I-90 and overshooting the exit for Sturgis by only twenty miles to the east. In terms of scenery, it wasn't much of a difference from the outbound route, but he discovered for himself what most long-haul drivers know: any difference is an improvement over the same old crap. It was late, past midnight, when he finally pulled the van into Calley's driveway, calling Gene twenty minutes beforehand so that he could come back to headquarters and open up the barn. Calley and Obregón were off again somewhere; Bobby had just enough brain power left to grab his duffle bag and stumble into the house to bed. He was not alert enough to remember the weed in the lockbox.

The Power and Rules

> *… but he himself has the power and rules.*

It was Thursday evening in Ann Arbor, a quarter after seven, in fact. Mac could tell by looking at one or the other of the two digital clocks in front of him, one on his kitchen range and one on the microwave above it. Behind him a radio, hung below one of the cabinets, said the same thing. Time is an essential element of cooking.

He was making dinner, building a trio of simple dishes that combined to become his favorite meal, or at least one of them. If he was making some other favorite meal, then *that* was his favorite, in that corner of whichever Goddamn quantum universe it happened to occupy. Tonight it was loin lamb chops, brilliantly simple, beautifully raised, perfectly butchered, from a farm just over into Ingham County. In any universe, lamb was certainly his favorite red meat, regardless of any quantum silliness. Mac was baffled by people who'd grown to adulthood without ever having it, and he was irritated by others who claimed not to like it. How could you not like lamb? Most likely, all they'd ever tasted was overdone restaurant chops, slopped up with mint sauce.

This led him inexorably to thoughts of folks he considered to be food heretics. Junk food people they were, people who ate at so-called Mexican chain places with extruded meat fillings and sugary bread-like substances. They were the people who bought groceries at supermarkets where the produce and the meat and the wine and the fish came from countries aglow with nuclear waste and factory farms, places where the animals and workers were indistinguishable in their lives, dignity, and compensation. These ideas led him further on to a nexus of food shopping angst: Ann Arbor had its share of cheap supermarkets, but in Mac's eyes the devil was an expensive, garish national casino of so-called organic cuisine. Nearly ten years before, they'd inflicted themselves on Ann Arbor, and Mac never set foot inside. He told people to their faces that the real locals were the ones who never shopped there. The fact that the parking lot had been deliberately downsized by a zealot on City Council "to encourage people to take the bus" was another sore point. It had created a vast traffic problem at the nearest intersection, flinging desperate left-turners out onto the street, just where Mac had to pass in order to get out to the county jail or the sheriff's department. His face began to set into a fixed scowl, and his left hand began to cramp up.

He'd been more or less happy, a minute before, with four burners going, chops searing, the oven pre-heating. Cubed yellow potatoes were getting tender in a pot of water and chicken stock, more stock was reducing for a sauce, and a pan of olive oil and butter was getting ready to accept a batch of blue oyster mushrooms. He'd been staving off the pain in his arches by shifting his weight back and forth. Now he'd gone down that damn supermarket path again and pissed himself off. He tended to abstain from his pain medications during the day, until he was home and not out driving around in traffic. Now he'd had some, and they were helping, but karma, damn it, karma. Focus. As long as the supermarkets can't run the little stores out of business completely, let the bastards fool the fools. If you believe 'organic' on a package of something from China means anything, you deserve what you get.

His phone went off, playing the opening bars of *Octopus's Garden*. The line "I'd like to be under the sea ..." indicated a call from Colleen, an enthusiastic swimmer. The call was brief, just letting him know that she'd be home shortly. He'd barely hung up when it rang again, this time playing an excerpt from *Witchy Woman*. Mac had never been able to resist song parody, and his mind always transposed this old Eagles number into "Ooh, ooh, twitchy woman." From there to its being his ringtone for Jenn Langton was no long step, although he never let her know about it.

"Hi, Jenn," he said.

"Mac, sorry to call so late ..." she started. The stove's timer went off.

"Hold on a minute. I've got a hot pan here." Mac set the phone down, turned off the burner under the chops, and pulled them out onto a rack. Now nicely seared off, they could sit for a while until they and the potatoes went into the oven for their final ten minutes.

"Okay," he said, "I'm back. What's up?"

"Again, I'm sorry I called while you're cooking." Jenn had eaten Mac's cooking on occasion, and she wished she were visiting in person. Her own cuisine was utilitarian.

"No problem."

"Can you do a road trip tomorrow?" she asked. "The Sturgis cops spotted Hagland's pickup truck, parked at some kind of farm store. They drove by again just now, and it's still there."

"You're kidding?" said Mac. "That quick, they found him?"

"Well, not necessarily *him*, but it's definitely the right pickup truck. I guess it's been there for a few days."

"When you say 'farm store,' you mean like a roadside stand? For produce?"

"No, it's a farm with a convenience store out front. The officer said they sell beer and wine, doughnuts, coffee. And then there's some other kind of business, too, but he didn't know anything about that."

"Now, what in the hell would Hagland be doing ... well, no point in guessing. So you want to drive down there?"

"I talked to Doug ... Agent Markowitz ... and he wants to go with us. And the Sturgis police want to have somebody there, too."

"Sure. Yeah, Doug'd want to be there. That's even reasonable," said Mac, thinking that if Doug wanted to go along, he'd already vetted the idea and gotten it blessed by higher powers. "Did he talk about a time?"

"Yes," Jenn said, "He wants to meet us here, then take two cars to Sturgis. So we'd meet in the Briarwood parking lot and just get back on 94."

"Okay, how early?"

"It's two hours from here, at least," she said. "So we're thinking about nine o'clock. I could pick you up a little before that."

"Make it eight forty-five," said Mac. "Give us time to get coffee."

So the elusive Robert Hagland had turned up. In Sturgis. Or his truck had, anyway. Mac thought it over, but nothing made any more sense than it all had twenty minutes before. Sturgis? A convenience store? On a farm? At least his culinary snit was over with, forgotten in favor of something more immediate and at least possibly capable of solution. He reset the timer to go off when the potatoes would be ready, and sat down to rest his feet. The dog joined him, sighing as she clambered up onto the couch. Colleen got home, changed out of work clothes, and gave the Shepherd a quick walk around the block. It was a minute or two after eight PM when Mac put dinner on the table and the three of them sat down. Bobby Hagland was still four hours or more from Sturgis, stopping for gas somewhere near Terre Haute.

The young Fed and the old Fed, Andy Patel and Doug Markowitz, were slowly arriving at a working relationship. In return for not asking more than a few questions a day and for making sure they were sensible and necessary questions, Andy would get exactly as much information as Doug thought he needed to have. Administrative and logistic arrangements would either be left up to Andy or handed to him as something already set in place. For example, if Doug said that they would be leaving Detroit for Ann Arbor at seven-thirty, then seven-thirty it was, and there was no point in suggesting other times or asking why. Unlike earlier trips and meetings, though, he did get a brief description of the event and its objectives.

"We're going over to Sturgis," Doug told him. "We've got a line on that Hagland guy. Bring a vest." By vest, of course, he meant discreet body armor, not semi-formal wear or a flame-orange, down-filled hunting garment. It told Andy that Doug was now thinking of Bobby Hagland as potentially dangerous, that this trip might involve an arrest, and that he, Andy, should take any and all other measures he thought would be useful, short of offering to drive or pick the route. With that in mind, Andy made his plans for the day.

One of his grandfathers had been born in India, but the family came to America when that gentleman was three years old, and the majority of Andy's genome actually reflected German, Irish, and Austrian ancestry. Besides the Patel name and a head of very black hair, there was little about him that suggested Chennai. He was a wiry and young-seeming person, younger-seeming than his real age of thirty-two, and his work ethic was that of the US Marine Corps. He'd been in for four years, and he'd seen combat during the early days of Iraqi Freedom. The FBI had recruited him on the basis of his college grades and his service record, and if he had a certain amount of ambition, it was no greater than most of his peers. Doug's characterization of him as a hungry little prick was unfair and a product of the older man's jealousy of relative youth and good health. In point of fact, Doug didn't actually dislike Andy at all, any more than he disliked most people.

Andy's preparation for the Sturgis trip was mostly cop-like. He made sure he had handcuffs and a side arm, the vest Doug had mentioned, and both a phone and a push-to-talk radio. Personal comfort called for a bottle of water, a can of cream-and-espresso coffee drink, and a couple of power bars. And going back to his military habits, he signed out the Detroit office's single example of an M-14 assault rifle, in its hard-sided case.

Some people would argue whether the M-14 was truly an assault rifle. It did offer larger ammunition capacity than the infantry guns it replaced, and in its military configuration, it was capable of automatic fire. But it was heavy, it had a wooden stock, and it fired a full-sized rifle caliber round. In fact, it chambered the exact round Bobby Hagland had just hauled back from Arizona, the Winchester .308 / 7.62 NATO cartridge. Early in the Vietnam era when the US started switching to the M-16 and its many variants, the M-14 faded away, but it never quite vanished. The Navy and certain Marine units, for example, kept it because of its longer range, greater accuracy, and better destructive power. In the service, Andy had been trained in its use and recognized for his proficiency with it. As a Fed, he tried to have one on hand when anything even slightly dramatic came up, and this probably fruitless jaunt over into the rural parts of Michigan was as dramatic a trip as he'd had since he came up from Cleveland. He doubted whether he'd even get the gun out of the trunk, but he liked having an excuse to bring it along.

Heavy Missiles

… insuppressible tumult and heavy missiles …

For the first time in weeks, the sun was shining and the temperature was in a range you might expect at this time of the year. It was Friday morning, the thirteenth of April, and things were off to a slow start at the farm. Gene DeVoos and Jerry Bien got there at their usual early hour and opened the store, but Calley, Obregón, and Bobby Hagland were all sleeping in. For Calley, the evenings entertaining his Salvadoran colleague were vastly annoying, a genuine trial for a man who perceived himself to have outgrown a taste for carousing and running around from bar to bar. In truth, he'd never really had a taste for it, but by now, he rationalized his disinterest as an effect of advancing age and increasing maturity. And even if he'd enjoyed getting drunk and chasing skirts, he had to abstain in order to get Obregón safely back to the ranch.

Sergeant Obregón enjoyed the evenings very much, especially since they were mostly on Calley's nickel, and since he didn't have to do anything except pick the Rush Street destinations and, eventually, fall asleep on the return drive. He slept in gratefully, since his deals with Calley were by now agreed upon, and he could spend the last couple of days of his trip just having fun.

Bobby was exhausted from all the driving; he was never much of an early-morning guy, anyway. So the house was quiet for the first few hours of the day. Out in the store, Jerry Bien sat on a stool behind the counter, waiting for customers. Gene sat in a chair in the office, looking through the inventory system and getting ready to place orders for caffeine, sugar, tobacco, and alcohol. Gene had given the van a cursory check, just to make sure it actually had a load of something, but he'd done nothing more. Mike had indicated that it might just as well wait to be unloaded until both Bobby and Obregón were out of the picture. Because he had no reason to do so, Gene hadn't looked in the lock box; to his knowledge, there was still nothing in it, anyway.

At about ten-thirty, Mike Calley, who'd been lying awake for a while, rolled out of bed and headed for the shower. Mike had been completely taken up with Obregón and the deals they were planning; the Arizona trip was a side show, and once Gene reported that Bobby had the ammunition and was headed back, he'd set it aside as a topic of worry. Now, he spared it a thought. He should go look at it while his guests were still asleep and make sure ... "Son of a bitch!" He suddenly remembered the lock box and the money he'd left there. It had been gone from his mind for almost three weeks, and now he realized that his own absent-mindedness had allowed a bunch of not-well-accounted-for money to be driven around the country by a man he scarcely knew. Task one for the day would be to get those Euros the hell out of there and turned into dollars. *I must be getting old*, he thought.

Neither Jenn nor Doug Markowitz felt especially constrained by speed limits. They'd beaten their own estimates by twenty minutes, and they were now in the parking lot of the Sturgis Police Department, talking with officers Tracy Douglas and Brian Colton. Douglas explained the simple route to the farm, and Doug suggested his preferred approach to the visit itself.

He and Andy would deal with the house, Mac and Jenn would watch the store and Hagland's truck, and the Sturgis officers could drive around back of the barn and make sure nobody left that way. He said that there was no indication that anyone out there would be dangerous or armed, but Hagland might be, so keeping eyes open was recommended.

"Are you sure the driveway goes all the way back behind the barn?" asked Douglas.

"Yeah, I am. Andy, you got that picture?" Andy pulled out a print of a Google Earth image, showing a satellite's view of the farm and a cleared gravel space in an inverted L, extending from the road, past the house, and then turning left to end on the north side of the barn. "You should be able to drive right back there," he said.

"Great," said Douglas. "Well, let's go, then." They got into their respective vehicles, with the cops going first, and headed north out of town.

Instead of two, there were actually three police officers in the Sturgis car. Colton and Douglas were in the front seats, and in the back was Goose, formally Carl Gustav, a European-trained German Shepherd. Just coming up on four years old, Goose was not a drug-sniffer, but he was adept in tracking suspects and taking them down, decisively and very effectively. He weighed only eighty-five or ninety pounds, but he was completely fearless and totally unimpressed with humans up to and beyond three times his weight. Humans, in fact, he grouped into three discrete categories: good people, bad people, and the doggie equivalent of 'meh', people who were irrelevant. You got to be in the good group if you were Officer Brian Colton, a member of Brian's family, or somebody wearing a Sturgis police uniform. Outside that group, you were irrelevant, up to the moment that Brian pointed at you and said "Get him!" Then you were bad.

Shepherd owners know that ninety-nine percent of them are happy, friendly dogs, whether they're purebreds or a mix. They're wonderful companions, and they live up to and sometimes exceed the usual estimate that dogs are on an intellectual par with a two or three-year-old human. But if you've noticed that members of minority groups, especially young people, seem to fear them, dogs like Goose are the reason why. Police dogs seldom really get to attack suspects any more than human cops do, but they're used extensively to intimidate; they're trained to bark and lunge, distracting and frightening the subject. It makes submission to the human officers seem like a better alternative. And while a biped cop will stop a few paces away, draw a side arm or a Taser, and order you to get on the ground, a dog will charge in at top speed, preferably from your blind side, knock you on your ass, and start chewing on your extremities. If you point a weapon at the dog or strike at it, in almost every jurisdiction in the country that's the same as doing it to a human officer, and it can get you shot. For better or worse, usually for the better if you're the one holding the leash, a Shepherd is the archetypical police dog.

The other thing that dog owners know about dogs in general is that, like a child or an employee, they need motivation and reinforcement in order to know what the right thing is to do. Human culture is a sophisticated and complicated thing, and to function usefully within it, a dog needs training. Many dogs start out as food-focused, valuing edible treats as a reward for good performance. Professional trainers usually recommend what they call "fading the lure" or phasing out food rewards in favor of access to a favorite toy or verbal praise. Goose was a great performer and a quick study because, almost from puppyhood, he'd been rewardable with just praise. He was exceptionally smart, well beyond the norm for his age and breed, and it typically took just a few repetitions of "That's a GOOD BOY!" to steer him down a desired path. Snacks were fine — he wasn't a picky eater by any means — but he was perfectly happy with a pat on the back. He could have excelled at agility competition, could actually have been a herd dog, probably could have learned to hunt, but given his size and looks, police work was perfect for him. The career path was really quite a sweet deal: he'd put in another five or six years, then retire as a pet, probably living with Officer Colton's family and following in the paw prints of Gloria, a twelve-year-old ex-canine officer who was occupying that niche at the moment.

At the farm, Calley dressed quickly, pulling on his usual jeans and a T-shirt. He hung a slide holster and a Beretta nine millimeter on his right hip and covered it with a longish dress shirt, left untucked, the simplest and most comfortable approach to concealed carry, especially for a full-size handgun. This was just habit by now; he had no more reason to expect trouble today than any other day. He went downstairs quietly, through the kitchen, and out the back door.

The van was in the barn, and all the barn doors were locked, all three of them, the two for vehicles and the one sized for people. He was carrying a clumsy wad of keys, keys for the house, keys for the barn, keys for his SUV and another set for the van. He unlocked the human door and out of habit, unlocked and opened the barn's back vehicle door, too. Mike wouldn't have said "habit." For him, it was procedure, preparation for an escape if he ever had to escape, since the SUV was always parked just inside that back door. Today, it was an act of suicide.

He unlocked the van next, slid back the side door, and confirmed that he did have a full load of something, at least. From what he could see, the pallets were wrapped, and nothing looked obviously tampered with. If there was a problem, it would probably be malfeasance on the part of the seller, not Gene's mechanic friend. He shut the door, walked around to the other side, and knelt down, feeling pain in his knees as he looked under the truck. The box was there, of course, but closer to the right side than the left. He groaned as he got up, cursing Obregón and his late nights, and went around to the passenger's side again. Crawling under, worming around on his back, he got into position, reached up, and unlocked the box.

It had been a long time – back in Addis Ababa, in fact – since Mike had seen packaged quantities of controlled substances, and there was an instant's confusion when four plastic bags of marijuana fell out of the box onto his chest, mixed up with his roll of Euros. It lasted only an instant, though, and it was replaced with fury. *That miserable, dumb-ass little shit! Driving clear across the damn country in my van with a load of munitions, and he's got dope in my lockbox! I will kill him! I will fucking kill him! And I'll rip Gene's balls off, too! Did some background checking, my ass*!

The time it took Mike to get back out from under the van was just long enough to start him thinking about the reality of the situation. He had the Euros in his hand, and he shoved the roll into a jeans pocket without bothering to look at it. The weed was lying on the barn floor, under the van, and whether to dispose of it or conceal it or take it back into the house and force-feed it to Bobby, one bite at a time, seemed like the most important choice to make first. There was a broom leaning against one of the tarp-shrouded storage racks, and he grabbed it. Bending down again and again, feeling the pangs of early arthritis, he fished out the baggies and stuck them under a tarp, on a shelf full of high-capacity magazines and optic sights. He stalked out of the barn and back toward the house, intending to throw Bobby out on his ear, first, then raise Mary Hell with Gene. As he went in the back door, the little convoy of cops and Feds was nearing the turn onto Highway 215.

In Jenn's car, Mac was looking at a copy of the satellite image. "You know," he said, I think we should park off the road, across from the lot. We should be able to watch the store and that pickup truck, too."

"Block it in, you mean?"

"Not necessarily, just be in a position to go after him if he runs. If we park in the lot, we'll have to turn around to get out."

"You think he'll run?"

"I always think everybody will run ..."

Upstairs in the house, Sergeant Obregón sighed deeply and rolled over. He was a practiced, in fact accomplished, drinker, and he wasn't technically hung over. But he was sleepy, half awake, with just a twinge of a headache and no real reason to get out of bed. He was wearing an olive drab T-shirt and a similarly dark green pair of boxer shorts.

Next door, Bobby was still soundly asleep, lying under the covers, shoes off but otherwise still dressed. It had been too damn much trouble to do more than scuff out of his tennis shoes and throw off his jacket. He was deeply unconscious when Calley pushed the door open.

"Wake up, God damn it," Mike said, raising his voice enough to be heard by Obregón, but not initially by Bobby. "I said, wake UP!" he repeated, kicking the side of the bed. That got through the layers of sleep sufficiently to register, and Bobby opened his eyes. He saw Calley, a man he'd barely met but knew as something of an authority figure, standing a few feet away and exhibiting signs of extreme anger. This was a situation Bobby had experienced before, several times, in fact, going all the way back to middle school, and that was the core of the misunderstanding that was about to take place.

In Calley's mind, Bobby was a faceless pot-smoking punk who was too dumb to understand the basic requirements of operational security. He was also an employee, of sorts. He expected him to respond to the displeasure of a superior with fear, possibly denial, and eventually submission. However, to Bobby, Calley was a random human being, a couple of sizes smaller, older, and less physically fit, and he'd just woken Bobby up. Instead of fear, etc., Bobby's reaction was confusion and anger, expressed in a rapidly developing attitude. The conversation degenerated.

"What the fuck?!" Bobby asked.

"You are fucking fired! Get your ass out of that bed and off my property!"

"What are you talkin' about? I drove all over hell yesterday! I'm sleeping!"

"You are not sleeping! You're fired! I found your damn weed in my van, you stupid little bastard! Get the hell out of here now!"

"I ain't going anywhere until I get paid!" Bobby stated, his voice increasing in volume. He sat up, kicking back the covers. "You sons-a-bitches owe me for the trip!" He swung his legs over the edge of the bed, and Calley noticed for the first time that he was a big fellow. And he didn't seem to be reacting in the way you'd expect. Mike backed away a step, and his right hand went under the shirt, falling on the butt of the pistol.

"I said you're fired, and I'll decide whether or not you just walk away or whether you pay *me*," Calley said. Bobby wasn't hitting on all cylinders at the moment, but he did suddenly remember the money he'd taken, and that it was physically related to a place where, he also recalled, he'd put the dope. If this angry little boss-man was aware of the theft, too, he might be in real trouble. Maybe he should cut his losses. He stood up.

"You want me to go? Okay, give me my stuff from the van and I'll go. But not until I get paid!" He took a step forward, and mostly out of reflex, stuck his hand into his jeans pocket.

"Your stuff? You want your stuff? Your weed? You're crazy! You'll be lucky if I don't call the damn cops!" Mike was watching Bobby's eyes and not his hands, not having been a cop himself. If this had been an arrest proceeding, an officer would have been focused on the hands, keeping them in sight, ordering the subject to keep them out of his pockets.

"You son of a bitch, I want my Goddamn money!" Bobby shouted, and pulled the little .22 four-barrel out of his pocket, not really intending to, a little surprised at himself for doing it.

Mike was transported back to Addis, back to the day the local moron squad tried to break in. That was the first time he'd been in anything like combat and also the last time. It had not been a pleasant experience. Then as now, all he could think of to do was fill his hand, as they used to say in the westerns. The Beretta came out and up, almost together with Bobby's absurd little gambler's gun. The .22 fired once, whether Bobby meant it to or not, and its tiny lead hollow point smacked into the door jamb behind Mike. Mike had the advantage of more practice and more theory (he knew, at least, what the phrase "sight picture" meant, even if he didn't have one at the moment), and his first round ripped through Bobby's left upper arm, making a painful but not especially dangerous wound. Unfortunately for Bobby, it was instantly painful; he screamed, dropped the little pistol, and half turned to his left to grab with his right hand at the place he'd been hit. The movement took half a second, give or take, and that was just enough to move his upper chest into the path of Mike's second shot. The nine millimeter jacketed hollow point round nicked his sternum, deflected slightly, mushroomed, and destroyed his aorta.

The yelling and the shots got Obregón out of bed fast, and he picked up the .45 that Mike had loaned him. Out on the road, the police vehicles arrived. Being inside moving cars, none of the good guys heard the initial shooting except possibly Goose, who went suddenly alert. Over in the store, both Gene and the clerk, Jerry Bien, heard it clearly enough. Gene stood up, feeling for his own little carry gun, holstered on his right hip. Jerry ran back behind the counter and picked up the shotgun. Out of twelve creatures present, only two had any idea what was actually happening, and one of them was dying.

Things might have been less chaotic than they turned out to be if Obregón had correctly interpreted the situation. He was still half-awake. He hadn't met Bobby Hagland, didn't know of his existence, wasn't aware that anyone was using the other bedroom. Because he was still getting up and finding his gun, he didn't see the Sturgis patrol car as it drove into the driveway and around back behind the barn. Most important of all, his emergency reactions and concepts were grounded in the reality of life in El Salvador, not the American Midwest. He looked out the window and, when he saw a plain black sedan enter and block the driveway, he didn't interpret it as containing harmless visitors or a pair of law enforcement agents, but as the vehicle of a business rival, come to attack Mike Calley and his enterprise. He jumped to the conclusion that the shots had been Mike or one of Mike's people shooting at the folks outside, and he promptly fired three rounds right through the window glass at Doug Markowitz, as he got out the driver's side.

Obregón was a good shot, and if the gun's rear sight hadn't been out of adjustment, he might have hit Doug. As it was, the .45 shot to the left, and all three of his big jacketed slugs slammed into the roof of the car. Doug disappeared behind the open door, and before the Sergeant could shift his aim, the person on the passenger's side had bolted around behind the car and popped up the trunk. The trunk lid wouldn't stop a .45, necessarily, but it hid the target.

Obregón had been trained to count his shots and not to fire away all his ammunition without securing a resupply. He was now down to five left in the gun. He had one spare magazine in the pocket of his trousers, and he dropped to the floor, crawled over to where the pants were lying, and retrieved it.

Mac and Jenn, as Mac intended, parked across from the store driveway entrance, fifteen yards or so short of where Doug and Andy were now under fire. Both of them got out of Jenn's car in a hurry; Jenn crouching behind the left front fender, putting the engine block between herself and the shooters, Mac getting down into the ditch and hoping the rear wheel would stop hits from whatever kind of big loud gun that was, firing from somewhere to the right.

Mike Calley was just feeling his adrenaline slack off slightly when it went ballistic again from the sound of Obregón opening fire on the Feds. He didn't need to look out the window. He knew that if that certifiable lunatic in the next room had started shooting at something, things were miles out of control. He had a plan for just this event, and it was time to put it into play. He reholstered the Beretta and ran down the stairs.

Behind the barn, Douglas and Colton let Goose out of the car. The door of the barn was open, and they said, "Police" loudly and entered. If Calley had left it closed, they would probably have stayed outside, but the open door was another matter. As they walked in, they heard Obregón shooting at Markowitz. Doug Markowitz was now burning up the air with his own calls for assistance, and the Sturgis cops added their "Shots fired!" calls to their own radio frequencies. They split up and moved right and left in the semi-darkness, checking the van and Calley's SUV for occupants. Goose stuck close to Colton.

In the store office, Gene stood frozen at his desk, trying to decide what shots from the house could mean. He heard Jerry running across the display area, a pause, and then the unmistakable sound of the shotgun's action; the kid had just chambered a round. Right on top of that, there came three more shots and some yelling (Markowitz shouting into his cell phone). Jerry Bien was yelling, too, but Gene wasn't listening. He was moving, out the back door and through the parking lot, struggling to get his compact revolver out of its waistband holster and untangled from his shirt. He would have run straight south toward the trees lining the road, away from the farm and the barn and the things in it, since his overwhelming, all-ruling panic was related to a cumulative feeling of dread about guns and ammo and explosives and all that death-dealing stuff they'd been casually handling all these years. And now, something or someone or some agency had caught up with them and by God, he had to get the hell out, hide somewhere, get as far away as he could. But he had to detour, because Bobby's S-10 was parked right in the way. And so it was as someone unknown to them, coming from behind the suspect pickup truck and fumbling at something with his right hand, that Gene appeared to Jenn and Mac.

Neither of them had any idea who had just been shooting or where that person might be. The only human they could see, besides Doug and Andy, sheltering behind their car, was this stranger running at them across the parking lot, and as he got closer, he drew a gun. Gene had finally gotten the five-shot Smith & Wesson loose, and it was waving around in his right hand as he ran.

Both of the Ann Arbor people had immediately drawn their own side arms when the shooting started, Jenn her intermediate-sized Glock and Mac his compact 26. Both now had them pointed more or less in Gene's direction, and both were screaming at him to stop and drop the gun. But Gene was in such a surreal state of panic that he saw nothing, heard nothing, just kept coming. Jenn's finger froze in place; it wouldn't obey her nervous system's instructions to place itself on the trigger and pull. Mac popped up from behind the detective car, shouted "Stop!" again, and as Gene's gun wavered more or less in his direction, began firing.

At that moment, poor confused Jerry Bien opened the front door. He saw Gene running madly down the parking lot with a gun in his hand. He saw Jenn's car parked across the road, and he saw Mac come up from behind it, point a weapon at Gene, and shoot. *It's begun!* thought Jerry, and he brought the Mossberg to his shoulder, aimed it at Mac, and pulled the trigger.

A shotgun is a reasonable defensive weapon, especially in a retail store environment, when it's loaded with shot. Birdshot will kill if it hits an assailant squarely and at short range. Buckshot, large pencil-eraser-sized round balls, loaded several to a shell, will kill absolutely if even one of them hits an artery or a vital organ. But rifled slugs, huge blundering lead cannon balls intended to bring down deer, are horrifically destructive, wherever they hit. And it was with slugs, most unfortunately for him, that Gene had loaded the Mossberg, since he was not all that much of a firearms enthusiast and didn't really know the difference. Jerry's shot hit him as he crossed the line of fire between the store and Mac. It smashed his spine, severed his spinal cord, made hash out of his right lung, and killed him on the spot.

Mac saw Gene fall and assumed he'd hit him. In fact, none of the shots Mac fired came anywhere near his point of aim. One hit the S-10; one went arcing up over the store and hit a tree trunk, a quarter of a mile away; several just disappeared; and the last one gouged a furrow in the parking lot. Back in the store, Jerry didn't know what had happened either; he assumed that the enemy out there had gotten Mr. DeVoos, and he racked another round into the shotgun.

Crouched behind Doug's car, Andy Patel was trying to sort out the tactical situation. The first rounds had come from the house; he'd actually seen the shooter at the window. Now, nothing was coming from there, and he was solely occupied with getting the M-14 out of its case and into the game. He could hear Markowitz talking frantically to someone about backup, State Police support, helicopters, and so on. Andy, whose thinking was still conditioned by his military background, was more concerned with deploying the resources at hand, since even in the Marines, reinforcements often took a long time to materialize. As he smacked the rifle's magazine into place, he heard Mac's nine millimeter start firing, and as he looked in that direction, he saw Jerry Bien in the doorway and saw the Mossberg go off, pointed in the direction of Jenn's car.

The rifle Andy had in his hands was a civilian version, without full automatic fire. In law enforcement, that was not very important, and for Andy, it meant almost nothing. The gun would fire every time he pulled the trigger, and he could do that very quickly, getting back on target between each round. That's what he now did, three times in succession. The first of the thirty caliber bullets smashed into the side of the doorway, sending wood splinters, flakes of dry wall, and bits of window glass spraying across Jerry's face and the side of his head. The shot went on into the store, penetrated a cooler, and exploded a liter bottle of soda.

Jerry flinched back and away from the wooden shrapnel, just far enough to enter the path of Andy's second shot. It struck the stock of the shotgun, broke the gun in two, and made a bloody mess out of Jerry's right hand. He dropped the gun and flung himself back into the store, avoiding the third round. That one went through the door and out the side wall, and it eventually vanished in the plowed earth of a field. Shocked to the core, Bien curled up into a ball on the floor and waited, sobbing, for the foe to come and execute him.

As Mike Calley ran down the stairs and back toward the kitchen, he heard the firing in front of the store, the shotgun go off, and the high-velocity *cracks* from Andy's rifle. "My God, my God," he shouted, without actually meaning to. He was now extremely focused on his bail-out plan, concerned only with making it to the barn, driving the SUV like hell across the north field, and running through the woods toward his stashed Honda and its emergency supplies of cash and food. The ATF or the army or the CIA or whoever it was out there could have the farm, they could have Gene DeVoos, they could have it all, just as long as he could get clear and get away, away to the convenient off-shore spot that he and the Virginia lawyer had set up, where there were forgiving banks, knowing, impoverished judges, and sunny weather. As Calley banged out the kitchen door and ran across the gravel space toward the barn, Bobby Hagland finished dying.

Upstairs, Alejandro Obregón low-crawled down the hall toward the stairwell. He glanced into the bedroom and saw Hagland lying on the floor, but the man was obviously unconscious, probably dead, and therefore of no use and no interest. He kept on until he heard the second bout of shooting, and then he jumped to his feet. No place to be caught, he realized, with just one way out, and the best thing to do was find Calley and see what the plan was. Attack or retreat, either way, Calley would have a plan, he was the professional here. So the Sergeant ran down the stairs, reaching the first floor just in time to hear the back door slam.

In the barn, Douglas and Colton and Goose heard the next round of firing, and then, in a matter of seconds, a door closing hard and running footsteps on gravel. They stood, separated by ten or twelve feet, momentarily gripped by indecision. The person coming could be a cop or a bad guy. Then the barn's human-sized door was wrenched open, and a man came in.

Calley, coming in from the daylight, was temporarily unable to see in the half-light of the barn. He knew, of course, where his SUV was parked, and he took a few quick steps in that direction. But then, as he did so, the door to hell broke open and a certified demon leapt out onto him. He was knocked to the ground by a howling, snarling, biting creature of darkness, a savage predatory animal from the deep reaches of the human subconscious, in a word, Goose, responding to Colton's command to attack. The dog was in his element, taking a dangerous suspect down and focusing that person's attention on himself rather than on Goose's partner and best friend, Brian. Calley screamed and tried to push the beast away. With his right hand, he tried to get his gun loose, but it was snagged on the holster's retention strap. He clawed frantically at it, hearing only the dog's muffled roaring, muffled by his own left forearm, clamped in Goose's jaws and being shaken violently left and right. He was unaware of Colton's shouting, his orders to turn over, to keep his hands in sight, to stop resisting. All he could think of was the nightmare animal attacking him and his desperate need to arm himself. With a last, wild effort, he tore the gun loose and raised it. And the world ended.

Colton could see perfectly, his eyes having adjusted to the low light. He saw Calley trying to draw a weapon, he saw him succeed, and he saw it come up in Mike's hand. He fired two .40 caliber rounds from his Smith & Wesson M&P. One struck Calley in the throat, one in the forehead, and that was all there was to it.

Officer Tracy Douglas, standing to Colton's left, had been covering the action with the patrol car's shotgun. The dog would have been in his line of fire, and he couldn't intervene. But he whirled when another man came through the barn door. Douglas saw the weapon in his hand, brought up the gun and with one buckshot round in the chest, knocked Alejandro Obregón flat on his back.

Four people were dead: Robert Hagland, who might or might not be connected with a murder in Ann Arbor; Gene DeVoos, who was the largely anonymous son of a man murdered years back in some kind of real estate imbroglio; Mike Calley, who no one had ever heard of; and for God's sake, a non-com from the army of El Salvador! The barn was full of illegal munitions and there was a bit of marijuana. Oh, and some local kid in the store was probably going to lose a hand. Three serving law enforcement personnel plus a very unofficial retired detective had fired shots, and some of them had actually hit what they were shooting at. Everyone who might have had the faintest idea what was really going on was now dead and therefore not talking. It was, in Markowitz's colorful but precisely accurate phrase, an unbelievable clusterfuck.

For his part, Goose sat down and stuck out his lengthy tongue. He was pleased. He'd have preferred a bit of chasing, but the biting part had been lots of fun. He sat patiently, panting to cool off, waiting to be told that he was a good boy. From his perspective, it had been a great morning.

A Share of the Earth

A share of the earth as her own, and of the barren sea.

Back in Milan, Jenn finished up her search of Bobby Hagland's basement bedroom. There was nothing more to find than there had been before; it was a thoroughly ordinary room, showing signs of having been occupied by a thoroughly ordinary young man. She'd bagged up a few additional things; a cup that might have DNA on it, although they had plenty of Bobby's DNA if they needed it; a business card for a bar in Colon; one lone .22 caliber shell casing, from back under the bed, clogged with spider webs and dust. She walked back outside.

The Feds and the Ann Arbor presence and the Monroe County deputies, there mostly because it was the most excitement they'd had in a while, were all clustered around a small shed. They were looking very, very carefully through it, and she decided not to add herself to the cooks. Instead, she walked through the sliding doors into the barn. It had already been

174

searched, and she had no real plan except a vague hope that she might find something the others had missed.

She stood in the center of the large open building and following one of Mac's methods, just looked around. She looked at the floor: it was poured cement, stained with oil and topsoil, but without holes or gaps or hidden compartments. Someone had checked for that. She looked at the junction between the floor and the barn walls, broken only by the uprights and one or two items of furniture. A steel office cabinet stood against one side of the building. It had been checked very carefully, inside, behind, under, on top. She looked at the top of the walls, where they met the roof. All the way around, the headers made a two-by-four shelf; it had been examined, inch by inch, by an officer with a ladder. The ladder, in fact, was still there, leaning against the wall.

Jenn looked up at the prefabricated roof joists, triangular supports at equal intervals. Everywhere they came together and made a resting place, someone had looked. There was nothing left here to be seen unless someone better at looking than any of a set of professional lookers were to come and look. She went back outside. The sky was still clouded over, and somewhere over in the west there was a faint sound of thunder.

She looked at the barn's only door, a sliding door, with two solid panels that hung on a rail from each side. She walked up to it and reached over her head. With her arm fully extended, she came up two feet short of the rail. Jenn stepped back and looked around. There was nothing to see but the cement ramp up to the door, the damp, muddy ground on each side of it, and a wooden crate. The crate was standing with its open top upwards, its sides maybe eighteen inches tall. It was empty, and the inside surface of the bottom was relatively dry, as though it had not, perhaps, always stood with the open top upwards.

Jenn turned it over. The bottom was convincingly wet, and on it were — scuff marks? As though just possibly someone had stood on it? Probably someone had, a cop who'd used it to search the sliding door rails. But it might have been someone else. Jenn went back into the barn and brought out the step ladder. She leaned it against one of the doors and climbed up. She went up far enough to bring her head above the rail, looked along it, and then got down again quickly. She unfolded the ladder into its triangular form, moved it to the farther end of the door, and climbed back up.

When she came down, she walked rapidly to the shed where Markowitz was supervising the search. "Doug," she said, "Take a look at this." It was a plastic bag.

"What is it?" said Markowitz.

"I think it's money."

It was. It was seven hundred Euros in older, crumpled notes, stuffed in a baggie. It was very much like the money Mike Calley had in his pocket when they searched his body, and just like that money, it was heavily contaminated with cocaine.

A full week later, there was a meeting. It was hypothetically about next steps on the Garfield homicide, but with the vast and weighty mass of the Calley enterprise to tackle, the Feds were clearly going to punt the Rodney sideshow back to Ann Arbor. The team, augmented by Chief Fredricks and a silent, almost comatose superior of Doug Markowitz, sat around a table in the Detroit FBI office while Doug reviewed the cast of characters so far.

"So what we had down in Sturgis, as we see it, was a conspiracy related to arms and ammunition, maybe other technologies. The ITAR violations alone will take years to track down." ITAR meant International Traffic in Arms Regulations. If Calley's Business 2 had ever had a mission statement, it might have been "We make money by circumventing ITAR."

"We won't ever know, probably, what was going on when we just happened to drive up. I don't think anybody was tipped off. I think we interrupted something, and our two main guys, Calley and the Salvadoran person, panicked and started shooting."

"What about Hagland?" Mac asked.

"That's probably the hardest to explain. Andy?"

Patel leafed through a binder and found a ballistics report. "What the crime scene people say is that he was killed by a nine millimeter round from the gun Calley was carrying. There was a weird little handgun on the floor where his body was found, and a round, probably from it, stuck in a door jamb. The shot that took him out was fired from near that door. So the guess is, he and Calley shot at each other up there in that bedroom, and he missed, Calley hit."

"And we have no clue why?"

"No. The survivor, this Jerry Bien kid, says he never saw Hagland and almost never saw Calley. His boss was DeVoos."

"We believe that? Why did the boy start shooting, then?"

"Poor little jerk was coached by his father in a lot of militia-speak, as far as we can tell," said Andy. "When he was interviewed, he said he thought the war of liberation had started. His father's a real piece of work. But everything we could come up with confirms that he was just a clerk in the store. And the store itself was very clean."

"What doesn't exactly fit with your case," Doug went on, "is the lack of a lot of drug evidence. We have the contaminated money and the Latin American connection, but we think maybe the bulk of that business had to be going on somewhere else. Obviously, we'll be chasing that very hard."

"So what do you think about Rodney Garfield?" asked Jenn. "You think these guys were involved?"

"I'm not sure it makes a lot of difference what I think about that, anymore," said Doug, "It's really your call. But if I had to speculate, yes, I'd think Hagland did the intel for them on the boy, and Calley and maybe Obregón did the shooting. I say that because of Hagland's connection to him, and because those other two were serious operators, easily capable of something like that."

"And we think the motive was ...?" said Mac. He was trying not to smile, not to show his amusement at Doug's carefully phrased, verbose utterances, so unlike those of the cranky, taciturn old agent he usually was when the Brass weren't on hand.

"I don't think we'll find that out for sure. Everybody we know of so far who would know is dead." He let that thought hover in the air, along with the unspoken addition "not that the agency is responsible for that."

"And what about the other one, Gene DeVoos?" said Jenn. "Do you connect him up, too?"

"Yes, we do," said Doug. "Preliminary looks at the computers that were on the scene show that he kept records of some kind for Calley. Except those for the store, they're all encrypted in a way that, to my mind, shows that he was involved heavily in illegal activities."

"Why he basically staged a banzai charge at you two, we don't know," said Andy. "He was running away from or toward something. Ran right into the clerk's shotgun slug."

"All right," said Fredricks, "I guess we'll run the rest of the case on those assumptions, then. Jenn? Mac? Any objections?"

Neither of them had any that they were willing to discuss in public. The meeting concluded, and Jenn and Mac rode back to Ann Arbor together, as usual in Jenn's car. The conversation was one that Mac knew was coming and had prepared for.

"Mac, I'm sorry about freezing up, back there at the farm," she said.

"Forget it."

"No, really. I just left it up to you. I could have done something. I left it to somebody else."

"Well, you might want to quit doing that, I guess."

"Or I might want to quit, period."

"No. You shouldn't. You did good, finding that money. That made Doug's whole day. Traces of coke, foreign currency ... kept him out of trouble."

"How?"

"Hooked it all up with the stuff he'd been told to look for. Nobody told him to look for an arms dealer, which is what Calley was, no doubt. But you gave him Calley-pays-Hagland plus coke. That'll keep the Bureau busy for a solid year. Happy, happy."

"Have you ever had to shoot before?"

"Nope. Knocked a lot of people down, hit a guy with a stick once. But I'd never pulled the trigger."

"Are you ... relieved you didn't hit him?"

"Sure. Hell, yes. Saves a lot of trouble, a lot of paperwork."

Mac opened his portfolio, a zippered document case. "I brought you a video you might want to watch. It's kind of a self-help thing, about motherhood and parenting and careers. I want it back. I watch it myself now and then."

"You don't have any children," Jenn said.

"Yeah, I don't. Anyway, I'll put it in your bag." He dropped a DVD case into Jenn's large purse.

"What's it called?"

"Aliens."

Cerberos

The carnivore Cerberos, Hades' bronze-baying hound …

Little Willy McDivitt faced an interesting public relations problem. Although his brother had, in fact, been responsible for the destruction of the Rome arrangement and for ratting out an entire police department, the challenge was to make it appear that he had not. It would be enough, maybe, to simply change any perception that Big Willy was a rat; it would be better if he could be rebranded as a loyal and heroic soldier who was serving his time and keeping his mouth shut. True, he had emphatically *not* given up any of the people on the paying side of the scheme, just the recipients of payment. But that would not be enough. For one thing, an expensive, carefully designed operation had been shut down, and for another, a rat was a rat. Big Willy would not be safe, let alone trusted by anyone, unless a new story, complete with a visible manifestation, could be created. Like a fleeing suspect visibly tossing away decoy evidence, it was necessary to throw something down.

In order to make that happen, Little Willy needed two general kinds of information, and since he was Big Willy's brother, he had to remain at a certain remove from the mechanics of the intelligence collection. This was necessary to avoid any apparent conflict of interest and also to keep from becoming a target himself. He decided that a couple of levels of indirection would be sufficient.

First, he contacted a girl among his friends in Rome, a girl he had actually slept with but who was not connected formally with him. Nobody would see her and say, "That's Little Willy's girlfriend." Although she was not, herself, very closely involved with the coke business, she had a cousin who was, very closely indeed. What Little Willy asked girl A to find out for him, via girl

B, was the name of anyone who seemed to be concerned about the Rome whistle-blowing and who might be connecting Big Willy with it. These would be the people to receive the disinformation he planned on manufacturing.

The second thing he needed was a scapegoat. It wouldn't be enough to just point the finger away from his brother; it'd be necessary to point it somewhere else specifically. And since the main things that indicted Big Willy were that he knew details of the operation and that he was arrested shortly before it all blew up, the scapegoat should probably be someone who was also jailed along about that time and who might credibly be claimed to know things, too. As it turned out, he hit pay dirt almost at once.

It took less than eight hours for girl A to get back to him with not one but two names. These were people in the Rome area, long involved in the covert import business and both extremely irate about having their deal with the cops fouled up. Both of them had been heard to blame Big Willy.

And then, trying to keep to his routine and not seem to be preoccupied with anything else, he dropped in at a fast food restaurant north of Rome, where he typically met associates, friends, and acquaintances. Among those acquaintances — he would not have called him a friend — was a guy named Rodney something, an insignificant kid without even a street name. Little Willy remembered him as a big mouth, a mooch, never up to anything interesting. It seemed as though the young man hadn't been around very much, lately, though, and without thinking much about it, he asked Rodney where he'd been.

"I been in jail, that's where, Dog," was the answer.

"Oh, yeah? What for?"

"Drugs. And resistin'."

And so, right up to the end, Rodney's mouth and his fondness for inflating his image played him false. It was exactly what Little Willy needed to hear. It was March thirty-first.

It took less than two days to finish the preparation. Another person, another girl, in fact, found time to tell Rodney Garfield a few random things, supplied by Big Willy to Little Willy, about the Rome cops deal. These were simple, unimportant facts or half-facts, nothing new or startling, but things that you might know if you knew lots of other details, too. Rodney, in turn, talked about it to anyone who would listen, because that was his nature.

At the same time, the serious people were told by girl B via girl A that perhaps they might be wrong about who the informer had been.

And as a result, on Sunday, April eighth, a guy Rodney knew mentioned to him that there was a party the next night. Rodney should come. As usual, Rodney didn't have a ride, but the other guy offered to pick him up. On Monday the ninth, Rodney went out his bedroom window, walked to the end of the street, and got into an older Dodge van, waiting for him in front of a closed convenience store.

"You dig E, man?" said the driver.

"Yeah, I'll take a tab," said Rodney. He had never really had any ecstasy, but he wasn't going to turn down anything free. Since he had no idea what it should look like, he swallowed a tablet without knowing that it was actually the so-called date-rape drug. By the time he should have been asking about where the van was going, he was unconscious.

They stopped once, at a house in Ypsilanti Township, where the driver turned the van and Rodney over to a pair of Hispanic gentlemen. They took the unnecessary precaution of duct-taping Rodney's hands. Then the van drove on south and turned west, eventually reaching a stretch of Textile Road, bordered on both sides by undeveloped public land. There they stopped and took Rodney out and into the woods. They laid him down in a thicket twenty feet from the road, and shot him, once each, in the head. When the bleeding subsided, they wrapped the body in a tarp, took it back to the van, and drove on into Ann Arbor and the airport. In the morning, Rodney was still there, the van was in a chop shop in Detroit, and everyone involved was catching up on their sleep.

Beyond and Far

Beyond and far from all the Gods …

The capital of El Salvador is San Salvador, and in the city, the Zona Rosa is an island of money. Calley's Virginia attorney turned from his window and its view of the city's chaotic lights. The Pacific Ocean was due south, too far to see, even from the higher floors of a shiny new hotel. He set his sweating glass down on a coaster and began typing a message to a colleague in Singapore. He'd encrypt it before it was sent; decoded, the subject line would read "Citizenship."

Up north in Macomb Correctional, Big Willy McDivitt was sleeping a lot easier. The message that Rodney's death had formed was being heard in a lot of places, out in the western suburbs. In Canton and Taylor, on west to Willow Run and Ypsilanti, out into Ypsi township, and even in a few north side and south side neighborhoods of Ann Arbor, the interpretation was, "Keep your mouth shut." It was helped along, reinforced, and clarified by a few dropped hints here and there; for the most part, it was clear enough on its own.

Nobody else the Ann Arbor police could think of to interview had anything to say. Rodney Garfield slipped further and further into the background. The FBI chased the Calley enterprise down alley after alley, some of them with results, others with none. No giant depots of cocaine were found, although dealing anything in the communities around Metro

183

Airport got temporarily harder. Other things came up. For the agencies, there was a national election on the horizon, and loonies of one stripe or another kept issuing threats, vague or specific, against candidates. They all required checking into, just in case one of them might be more than a crackpot. In Ann Arbor, graduation and the general end-of-year loosening of standards brought on a rash of minor burglaries, just as it did every spring. And the festivals and fairs season was coming; once school was out, the city bloomed with street events of all kinds, all calling for policing, and all generating a low-level buzz of petty criminality. The cops were busy. And so, although the case remained in an unsolved state, the department became more and more inclined to believe that the perpetrators of Rodney's murder had all died in Sturgis, scattered around Mike Calley's farm.

Jenn didn't quit. She seemed at least a bit more relaxed, and one morning she taped a poster to the front of her desk; it was a promotional shot of Sigourney Weaver, holding an assault rifle.

April passed and the weather got better. May Day was a Tuesday, and Mac was having a less pleasant morning than usual. He'd stopped calling them 'bad', since just being up and dressed and with a cup of coffee in hand was so much better than the alternatives. But still, he wasn't a healthy, contented man. Joints hurt, and his sinuses were annoying. He was groggy from waking up in the small hours with muscle cramps. His ambition was idling somewhere near zero.

He sat on the couch in the front room and thought about how much he enjoyed couches lately. You could sit on a couch and read, you could sit and just stare out the window, and if it seemed like the right thing to do, you could stretch out on the couch and fall asleep. Right now, though, he was still alert enough to think about Rodney and Rome and Sturgis. Mac and Jenn Langton had hashed it over, at length, separately and apart. Everything they knew pointed at a connection with Calley and Hagland, but the trouble was, they knew so damned little. None of the guns from the farm matched up with the projectiles that killed Rodney. That might mean one thing or another, though; it might just be another aspect of the shooter's professionalism, having disposable guns and disposing of them. They were willing enough to use force, witness the shootout itself, but they hadn't been very effective. Some of them, at least, seemed to have panicked. *But if you turn that around*, Mac thought, I'm *supposed to be a professional, I started shooting, and I didn't hit a damned thing*.

Not too long ago, Chief Fredricks had asked Mac, "So what do you *really* think about it?", and Mac had told him, "I think we don't know enough, and I think we never will." With that thought, he got close to the core of it, but the essence still slipped through his hands: no one involved knew enough, not Calley about Hagland, or DeVoos about Calley, or Rodney about life in general. And what you don't know can kill you.

The sun coming in the window warmed a patch of the couch, and Mac decided on a nap. He stretched out, closed his eyes, and thought: *All you have to do is turn your back – hell, just blink – and you're old and broken. It all happens in the blink of an eye.*

End

185

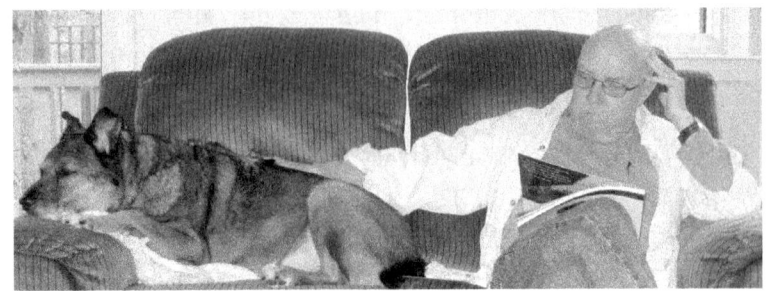

Author photo: L. Bangert

*Joseph McConnell describes himself as a retired technical bureaucrat. In and around his day jobs, he's been writing for decades, once sharing the cover of Whole Earth Review with Allen Ginsberg. Born in (extremely) rural Michigan, he's lived in Ann Arbor since 1977 and — whether the city is prepared to admit it or not — considers himself a stakeholder. **Many Believable Lies** is his first novel.*

Other books by Joseph McConnell:

Clash by Night

The Least Weasel